D1403113

DONOVAN'S GUN

Also by Luke Short
in Thorndike Large Print

Sunset Graze
And The Wind Blows Free
Play A Lone Hand
The Man On The Blue
Ambush
First Campaign

DONOVAN'S GUN

LUKE SHORT

Thorndike Press • Thorndike, Maine

16.95 12/90 Pub.

Library of Congress Cataloging in Publication Data:

Short, Luke, 1908-1975.
  Donovan's gun / Luke Short.
    p. cm.
  ISBN 1-56054-078-8 (alk. paper : lg. print)
  1. Large type books. I. Title.
[PS3513.L6815D66   1990]   90-11289
813'.54—dc20   CIP

Thorndike Press Large Print edition published in 1990
by arrangement with H. N. Swanson Agency.

Cover design by James B. Murray.

The tree indicium is a trademark of Thorndike Press.

This book is printed on acid-free, high opacity paper.

DONOVAN'S GUN

1

Jim Donovan, mounted on a dusty bay gelding, was picking his way through the midday horse-and-wagon traffic of Pitkin, when he heard the shrill whistle, followed by the call, "Hey, Jim!"

He was just past the River House, a big two-story brick building that faced the river across the street, and now he turned his head in that direction. Case Harvey, bull-big in shirtsleeves, raised a meaty hand in a beckoning gesture, and Jim, letting an approaching wagon pass him, kneed his horse around and headed for the roofed portico of the hotel. His gaunt weather-browned face reflected impatience as the blast of the sun of this July day hammered at him.

Reining in before the portico, he sat motionless, a tall, high-shouldered man of thirty dressed in a faded calico shirt, wash-softened levis and scarred cowman's boots. His horse shook his head, jangling the bit as if he were as impatient as his master.

Case Harvey, hatless, his meaty face flushed with the heat that was everywhere, came up and halted beside Jim's horse, tilted his head and said in a gravelly voice, "He's in the barroom."

Jim raised a hand to lift off his dust-colored Stetson and wiped his sweaty forehead with his forearm. His dark straight hair was sweat-matted and needed cutting, and beneath it his lean face took on a wry look.

"Where else would he be?"

"We broke up the game after daylight. Cole stayed on for a nightcap but I went to bed. He's sleeping it off at the front table."

A faint amusement replaced the impatience in Jim's grey eyes. "You run out of rooms, Case?"

"No, the swamper's just a kid. When he woke Cole he tried to fight him, so the kid let him be."

"He lose again last night?"

Case dipped his head. "Like always."

"Got his I O U on you?"

"No, but you'll see it tomorrow along with the rest of 'em. It's tomorrow, ain't it?"

"Eleven o'clock, my office." Jim lifted his reins. "Let him sleep, Case. I'll pick him up later."

Jim kneed his horse around, crossed River Street to its shady side, and headed in the direction he had been going before Harvey whistled him down. The stage from Primrose crossed the bridge over the Cheat ahead, turned down the street and passed him, headed for the River House. It left a curtain of dust in its wake that Jim held his breath against for a few seconds.

Pitkin's first settlers had had the foresight to hack the town out of a vast cottonwood motte, sparing many of the trees, so that huge cottonwoods shaded the whole four blocks of River Street on the river side. Keeping in this shade, Jim rode down to the middle of the next block, then put his horse in at the tie rail opposite the *Banner* office. It was a narrow red-painted, false-front building, wedged in between Lyall's butchershop and Woodward's hardware store.

Jim dismounted in the shade, feeling the faint cooling breeze coming off the Cheat River. He looked at the *Banner* building with something close to a scowl, and then picked his way through the heat-slowed saddle-horse and wagon traffic. Most of the buildings on this block had wooden canopies jutting over the plank walk, and the *Banner* building was one of them. Jim ducked under an empty tie rail and achieved the boardwalk, and then headed for the double doors of the newspaper office, which were flanked on either side by wooden benches.

Inside, immediately in front of him, was a

9

high scarred counter with a gate in its middle. Behind the counter, seated at a big paper-littered, flat-topped desk, sat a young woman of twenty-six who, in spite of her youth, was the *Banner* owner and editor. At the moment she had a pencil wedged between her teeth and was furiously erasing something from a paper on her desk. The creak of the opening gate made her look up, and her hand stilled before she lifted it to remove the pencil. The action straightened out the grimace in her face, leaving, as she recognised Donovan, an expression of good-humored mockery, mingled with surprise.

As Donovan pushed forward and let the gate slam behind him, Kate Canaday said, with dry mischief in her voice, "Why, Counselor Donovan! Are you sure you have the right place? Are you sure you won't feel contaminated?"

"I already do." His voice was curt. "Am I too late to get a legal notice in this week's *Banner?*"

"Why, for you we'd work all night," Kate said mockingly.

"Got paper and pencil?" Regarding him warily with her green eyes, Kate reached up to her chestnut hair, piled on top of her head, took out a pencil which was tucked there, and reached across her desk for a sheet of copy paper. She was wearing paper cuffs to protect the sleeves of her drab grey dress, over which she was wearing an ink-stained canvas printer's apron. The last time he had seen her was at Burt Hethridge's funeral four months ago. This was a girl he disliked so much he avoided having anything to do with her, always doing necessary business by messenger.

He accepted the paper and pencil, sought a clear spot in the desk's litter and wrote down his notice. Finished, he tossed the pencil on the desk and gave the girl what he had written.

She glanced at it briefly and then lifted her glance and looked at him, her eyes again mocking. "You could have saved yourself a trip, Counselor. Your notice to creditors of the Hethridge estate is already set up."

"Who told you to do that?"

Kate smiled faintly. "I've worked on this newspaper longer than you've been a lawyer, Jim Donovan. One of the first things I learned when I began to set type was that legal publications come in threes or sixes. This is the third and last notice to Hethridge's creditors, so it's already in the forms."

Jim said with disgust, "Damn!"

Kate waited an impassive moment. "Or God damn, maybe. Which?"

"Both."

Jim raised his glance and looked past the

low railing behind her desk at the shop. Rich Sturdivant, her printer, stepped from the type case to the composing stone, over which a lamp burned. He elbowed his young printer's devil out of the way and then considered the form on the stone. Jim saw, but registered none of this; he was thinking that this was a wasted day, totally wasted. He was angry with himself, and for an old reason, angry with Kate Canaday.

Kate's voice brought his attention back to her, when she asked, "Now just what did we do wrong?"

"I sent a message over with a legal notice earlier in the week. You could have told him the Hethridge thing was taken care of."

"Yesterday was one of your days in town. You could have stopped by and asked," Kate said tartly.

He eyed her coldly. "I could, but the less I have to do with you the better."

"I agree with you, but it seems we need each other. You're required to publish, and I have the only paper."

Jim nodded. "Well, that's the last money you'll make off Burt Hethridge. God knows, you've made enough off him already."

"Not too much," Kate said mildly. "The *Capitol Times* doesn't pay its stringers very much."

"Except when they get a cheap, lip-licking story like the one you sent in when Burt died."

Kate flushed, and there was anger in her green eyes as she said, "I only wrote the truth about his death."

"Sure," Jim said derisively. "He died in a sporting house. What if he'd died in a privy? Would you have written that?"

"That's not the same thing, and you know it," Kate said angrily. "He was one of the wealthiest ranchers in the state. Two grown children, pillar of the community and all that. What was he doing at Minn Daly's?"

"His own damned business and none of yours."

"You're right, it was a damned business. I just wrote the shameful facts, and they were shameful."

"Well, you made it a little hard for the preacher at his funeral sermon. You made it pretty close to impossible for the women friends of his dead wife. You made his daughter feel fine, just fine." He dropped the irony now as he said, "But the people you made happiest were his enemies. You robbed his death of all its dignity." He paused. "I've been wanting to tell you that for a long time. How much do I owe you" he asked, and added, "In money, I mean."

13

Kate, still flushed under his tongue-lashing, said, "I'll bill you."

Jim turned and, not bothering to say goodbye, went through the gate and out the door, his rage still smoldering. He hadn't intended to say what he had said, but now that it was out he was glad of it. Halting on the boardwalk, he looked at his horse and decided to leave him there in the shade rather than ride him up to the River House and tie him in the sun.

He headed for the River House, his anger ebbing. Perhaps the day had not been a total waste, since he had spoken out to Kate Canaday. This morning he and one of his two punchers had started to push his D Cross cattle onto higher range that he had leased in the Longbows, and they had been four hours in the saddle when he realized he had forgotten that the publication of notice to creditors for Burt Hethridge's estate was due for publication in tomorrow's *Banner*. As executor of the estate, he knew it was too big to be jeopardized by technical flaws in its handling, so he cut for town. Needlessly, Kate Canaday had just told him.

Recalling their exchange of words, he regretted not having said that if she had been a man, he would long ago have pulled her out on the street and beat her up for publishing

14

the details of Burt Hethridge's death. Still, she probably knew that and took advantage of the fact that she was a woman. What in hell was she doing publishing a newspaper, anyway? Why hadn't she sold it and taken a job teaching school, as an ordinary young woman would have done?

He remembered her father then, a likeable, hard-drinking Irishman. Twelve years ago Mike Canaday had come to Pitkin with his motherless daughter to work as a printer for the *Banner*. Jim remembered that after school hours Kate Canaday had worked as a printer's devil, and that was an unheard-of thing for a girl to do. When he was in law school, Jim learned that Canaday had bought the *Banner* and was making so good a thing of it that he had purchased a small house in town. Two years after Jim had hung out his shingle in Pitkin, Mike Canaday had died and Kate had taken over the *Banner*. They had got on amicably enough, maybe because he was so busy dividing his time between his law practice and his small ranch that he saw nothing of her except in the way of business. Besides, while she was pretty enough, she was an unregenerate tomboy who worked as hard at her job as he did at both of his.

Her story of Burt Hethridge's death, which was published not only in the *Banner* but in the *Capitol Times*, had turned his amiable tolerance of her into an active dislike. Even in Burt Hethridge's obituary, carried in the same issue of both papers, there was little about the man. Nothing was said in either that he started out an illiterate cowboy from Texas. While both mentioned he was a controversial figure, a tough rancher who ran a tough crew, neither mentioned how wonderfully generous he was, and that he had sent half a dozen boys through college, one of them Jim Donovan.

At the River House Jim entered the lobby and headed for the entrance of the barroom on his left. Crossing the carpeted lobby, he glanced over to the desk to his right, expecting to see Case Harvey. However, there was no one behind the desk, and he moved into the barroom. It was a small room with a round card table and chairs on either side of the door, and the bar against the back wall. Otey Bliss, the bartender, was a small, spare man of fifty, egg-bald, with a face the sun had long ago wrinkled but which now had the pallor of an indoors worker. He was talking to a whiskey drummer who had his order book on the bar in front of him. Jim raised a hand in lazy salute and then glanced toward the table nearest the street.

As Case Harvey had said earlier, Cole Hethridge, head on crossed arms, was sleeping; a

16

half-empty bottle of whiskey and a glass stood just beyond his head with its cap of blond tightly curled hair. He was, Jim noted, dressed for town in a white shirt with ruffles, underneath a red flannel vest.

Jim moved up to the bar and when Otey came over asked for a beer. When Otey placed it before him Jim asked, "Any more trouble, Otey?"

Otey shook his head. "The bottle took care of that."

Jim took his beer and moved over to the table, set the glass down, then put a hand on Cole's shoulder and shook it roughly.

Cole Hethridge roused, straightened his back and looked up sleepily to see who had wakened him. When he saw Jim he said in a thick voice, "Oh, it's you."

Jim pulled out the next chair, sat down and silently regarded the slim young man beside him. He was twenty-four and handsome, but he had the drink-slackened face of a man ten years older. His loose, full-lipped mouth always settled into sullenness when he wasn't talking or smiling, but then he was usually doing both. His looks were so different from his homely, taciturn father's that it was hard to believe Cole was Burt's son. His tightly curled hair was the kind women loved to stroke, and a lot of them had done so. His bloodshot eyes were of the deepest brown and he rubbed them now with thumb and index finger of his right hand, as if to erase the drunken sleep from them.

After shaking his head, Cole drew a watch from the pocket of his red flannel vest. The vest had gold buttons, which Jim knew were really gold.

Cole looked at the watch and said, "You're only three hours late, Jim."

"You ought to carry a calendar instead of a watch, Cole," Jim observed. "We were to meet tomorrow."

Puzzlement came into Cole's face as Jim continued, "Tuesdays, Thursdays and Saturdays are my office days, which you damn well know." He gestured toward the bottle. "You must have gained a day out of that stuff."

Cole frowned. "Today's Thursday, else why are you in town!" he asked flatly.

"It's Wednesday," Jim countered. "I came in to check the notice to your creditors in tomorrow's paper. I want you on hand in my office at eleven o'clock tomorrow. That's what tomorrow's date was all about, remember?"

"Pay 'em off," Cole said sullenly. "It isn't as if we didn't have the money."

"It's not that easy, Cole. Gamblers don't bill you the way a hardware store does. Why, the money you owe Case Harvey would build him a new wing on this hotel. Lord knows what you owe Tom Dunning down at the Cameo. When they read this notice, which is their last chance to collect, they'll come to me because I'm executor. I want you on hand to confirm or deny that you owe the sums they say you do."

"I probably do," Cole said dryly. "With the allowance you put me and Sis on, I have to borrow money even for cigars."

"I haven't heard Sarah complain."

"A new dress every other month would keep her happy," Cole said scornfully. "But a Baptist minister couldn't live on what you give me."

"That's my job, Cole. The court thought your allowances were reasonable." He added, "Anyway, I won't be riding herd on you much longer. Once your debts are paid out of the estate, then you and Sarah are on your own."

"Gee, maybe I'll buy a new hat," Cole said sardonically.

"You'll have enough money to buy the factory if you want."

Cole folded his arms and leaned forward, regarding Jim with cold appraisal. "How much are we worth, Jim?"

"You and Sarah thinking of liquidating?"

"No, I just want to know what Triangle H is worth."

"If you can hold onto it, you mean."

Cole gave a short bark of a laugh. "We'll hold it. Those out-of-the-pants nesters don't scare Will-John or the crew."

"Do they scare you?"

"No, why should they?"

"I just wondered. They scared your father, although he'd never admit it."

Cole reached out for the bottle and poured himself a drink. This reminded Jim that he hadn't touched his beer, and now he drank half of it in three thirsty swallows. After Cole had taken his drink he set down his glass and said, "Why would he be scared of them?"

"Because he'd hurt them, time and again. Just like Will-John's doing now."

"All we've done is hold the range we've always claimed."

"And you've claimed too much."

Cole gave an impatient wave of his hand. "I don't want to talk about it, Jim."

"Neither do I. I never even liked to talk about it with your father. But I keep remembering something your father said once."

"You're always quoting my father," Cole said derisively. "All right, quote him again."

"Here it is, then. 'No man is so poor he can't own a gun, and anybody will loan him a cartridge.'"

Cole frowned. "What's that supposed to mean?"

"It can mean anything you read into it."

Cole regarded him broodingly for a moment, and then he laughed. "Old sunny Jim Donovan," he said sarcastically. "Always cheerful, always loveable, always right."

Jim's dislike of Cole bordered on anger now, but he checked himself. *Just one more day and I'll be shut of him,* he thought. He made no comment.

"You never answered my question, what's the estate worth?"

"It's what anybody will give you for a hundred odd sections of land, five thousand head of beef, two hundred and fifty head of horses, two ranch houses and half a dozen line shacks. I just can't tell you, Cole. But there's one thing I can tell you."

"You've been telling me for months, but go ahead. Say it again."

Jim smiled crookedly. "All right, you and Sarah can't spend all of your yearly income if you live the way ordinary, prosperous people live. But if you want to take on every gambler this side of the Mississippi, you could lose it all in a year." He added dryly, "Hell, it doesn't take any brains to spend money, Cole. Almost everybody will help you spend it."

"Starting with you?" Cole asked.

Jim felt anger surge up in him and he said quietly, "Little man, watch out. You've picked the wrong day to lean on me. I've told you I'm not charging a fee for this job. If the court awards me one, I'll return it. Not, you understand, because of my deep affection for you. You just happen to have had a father I admired."

2

It took Beau Cather a full day to get word to the three men he wanted. That word was for them to meet at his place on the edge of the Hornsilver Breaks the following day, which was this same Wednesday.

Long before noon of this sunny day, they were assembled on the porch of his mean shack at the base of a clay slope which verged on land that was such sorry graze Triangle H hadn't bothered to claim it. The three men Beau had called in were of a type, as was Beau. They were in their late thirties, dressed in the shabbiest of range clothes, not recently shaven, and they arrived on poor horses. To describe one was to describe all four. They had the air and appearance of beat, resentful men.

The fifth man was a different breed of cat. He was in his early thirties, wore newer and cleaner range clothes, and rode a good horse stolen especially for this trip. To each of the three as they arrived singly that morning,

23

Beau had introduced him thus: "This here's the boy I sent for. Name's Keefe Hart."

After Beau had introduced Hart to Shorty Linder, the last of the three, he went into his one-room shack and returned to the porch with a gallon jug of pale yellow moonshine that was three-quarters full. Hart lounged on the dirt floor of the porch, his back against one of the posts. A barrel chair, wired to hold it together, had been reserved for Shorty, who now sat in it. Davy Forsyth, taller than the others, shared a bench with Arly Green, a gaunt and excessively dirty man.

Beau placed the jug on the floor between Hart and Shorty and then sat down on the chopping block. His pants were so thin he could feel every axe mark and he made a mental note not to move too quickly for fear of picking up a splinter. Beau had impudent blue eyes that would, in a more prosperous man, have indicated a fun-loving disposition. In Beau they reflected only a resentment against all men and all life.

When the jug of moonshine had been ceremoniously sampled and passed around it wound up with Beau, who took a swig that gagged him before he put the cob cork back and set the jug beside him.

Beau began by saying, "Well, I'll tell you boys the word I sent Hart. See if it's the word he got." He looked at Hart. "I said if you could get one man out of the way we could cut up Triangle H like it was plum pie. Is that the word you got, Hart?"

Hart nodded, almost indifferently.

"So you're here, and that means you'll do it."

"My letter say that?" Hart drawled.

"Your letter said you'd be here this mornin'."

"Triangle H is a pretty big spread," Hart said. "I rode all day yesterday and I was never off'n it. Sure I'd like a piece of it, but tell me how I get it."

"It goes like this," Beau said. "When Burt Hethridge died he left the spread to his two kids, a boy and a girl. They're both in their twenties. The boy is a drunk, the girl's a stuck-up old maid. The whole outfit is held together by the ramrod, name of Will-John Seton. Get him out and we move in. That's all there's to it."

"Then why don't you do it?"

Beau shook his head and smiled. "Triangle H has got close to forty hands on their two spreads. Any one of us makes a move and we're dead. It takes somebody from outside."

"Can't they make him just as dead?"

Shorty Linder said in a surprisingly bass voice, "Not if they don't catch him."

25

Hart frowned. "So I take Will-John Seton out. They hire a new ramrod."

"Not like him," Beau said.

"Why is he special?"

Beau leaned forward, elbows on his knees, and said, "Will-John was old Burt Hethridge's fair-haired boy. He taught him the country and taught him how to ramrod two big outfits. He's mean and tough and a hustler."

"So are a lot of ramrods," Hart countered.

"There ain't a man on the Triangle H crew that could handle Will-John's job. That means the Hethridges would have to go outside for a good man. Before he could begin to learn the country, we'd be at him."

"He'd still have those men behind him."

"Don't you believe it," Beau said flatly. "Once the bushwhacking starts, they'll drift. Why would they stay and buy a shot in the back just for a new ramrod, a drunk kid and a sour girl?"

"So this Will-John holds it all together?" Hart mused.

Gaunt Arly Green said quietly, "You betcha. This here Will-John has a stake in Triangle H, and that's what makes him the hard man he is. Hethridge staked him to his own beef. They eat Triangle H grass and Triangle H hands work them. So when he fights to hold Triangle H range he's clawin' for his-

26

self. No new ramrod could get that kind of a deal. It's somethin' you got to grow into, like Will-John did."

"Will-John got a *segundo?*" Hart asked.

"Two of 'em," Beau said. "But they've got no stake in the spread. They're paid five dollars a month more than the ordinary hands, and that ain't worth a shot in the back to any man."

"How many boys you got?" Hart asked. "Just this many?"

"We got a dozen more," Beau said. "Once Will-John's gone, they'll show."

"They got it cut up for theirselves already?"

"No. We got enough men to say who gets what, and make it stick."

"What's the law like here?"

Beau said, "Old boy name of Harry Andrews, a Triangle H man. Without a crew to back him up, he's nothin'."

"Any deputies?"

"Two nephews of his. Nothin' to 'em."

Beau picked up the jug, rose, moved over and wordlessly handed it to Hart; then he returned to his chopping block and gingerly sat down. Hart took a drink, passed the jug to Shorty and wiped his mouth with the back of his hand. When he could talk he said, "Sounds like this Will-John makes pretty big tracks."

Beau nodded. "Like I said, he's all that

27

holds Triangle H together."

"Where can I find him?"

"Don't go lookin' for him," Beau said flatly. "We'll point him out to you."

Hart said, almost lazily, "Let's talk pay."

"No money, because we ain't got any," Beau said. Once we're on top, your share is four sections of the best graze and what they call Number Two ranch."

"Any stock go with it?"

Beau grinned mockingly. "Why, Mr. Hart that'd be stealing. What we're after is a chunk of open range enough for all of us to make a living off of. Ain't that enough for you?"

"I reckon," Hart said idly. "Now show me this Will-John."

"Then it's a deal?" Beau asked.

"Sure as you're born."

Beau stood up now and said, "We go into Pitkin. That's the county-seat town, five miles west. There's a saloon there, name of First Chance. They got rooms up above the saloon. Shorty'll go in with you. A couple of times a week Will-John Seton comes to town. Every time he does he hits the First Chance, because that's where most of us hang out. When we're in town, he comes in and buys us a drink, just to show he ain't afraid of us. Shorty will point him out to you, but he really don't need to. When you see him, you'll know him."

28

3

On that same Wednesday afternoon, two blocks back of the River House, Will-John Seton sat in the kitchen of a one-story frame building abutting the boardwalk. A sign on the building jutted out over the walk, bearing the legend:

BONNIE LEAL
DRESSMAKING
MILLINERY

A card edged in the side of the half-glass door said, "Closed till 5.30." It had been put there only moments before by Bonnie Leal, who was now taking a granite-ware coffeepot from the black iron kitchen range in the rear room of the building.

Will-John Seton, a wide-shouldered, deep-chested man of thirty, slacked loosely in his chair, legs straight out, booted feet crossed at the ankles. As Bonnie turned with the coffee-pot in her hand, Will-John raised his hand, palm out and said, "No more, Bonnie. God, you must have made that coffee last month. It could float a horseshoe."

"Maybe you'd like it poured down your neck," Bonnie said tartly. She was a small girl with tousled black Irish hair, and blue eyes so pale they were almost grey. She was wearing a grey smock over her dark red dress. Where her high full breasts bulged out the smock, there were a dozen pins, and draped around her neck and trailing down the front of the smock was a cloth tape measure. She was dressed just as Will-John had surprised her a few minutes ago in her front-room workshop with its dummies, cutting table and sewing machine. A pretty young woman of twenty-seven who was aware of her attractiveness, she went now to the kitchen table, refilled her own cup and then looked enquiringly at Will-John.

"I've got some milk you could put in it."

"No, thanks. The milk will only curdle."

Bonnie made a face at him, and moved to put the coffee-pot back on the stove.

Will-John watched her appreciatively. His straight dark hair was as black as Bonnie's and his high-bridged blade of a Roman nose separated eyes that were amber as a cat's.

Bonnie came back to the table and sat down. She was lifting her cup of coffee to drink when Will-John asked, "Cole still stay-

30

ing away from you?"

Bonnie took a sip of the coffee, put down the cup and said, "It's more like I'm staying away from him. He comes around but I won't let him in."

"That's why he's boozing it up?"

"Does he need a reason?" Bonnie asked dryly.

"Well, he's feisty with everyone," Will-John said. "He and Sarah are just barely speaking. Yesterday I had to cuff him for taking a chain to a horse. If that's what love does to you — no, thanks."

"Well, a preacher can always end this."

"If you had to bet, Bonnie, how would you bet?"

"I'll get him," Bonnie said softly. "I'm in his blood, Will-John. It'll just take time."

"Jim Donovan's paying off Cole's creditors tomorrow. By next week the estate will be settled. He's there for the picking, Bonnie." He frowned now as if struck by a sudden thought. "What if I started taking you out? There's a dance Saturday night at the Masonic Hall."

Bonnie shook her head. "It's way too risky, Will-John, and you know it. He'd only fire you, and then where are we?"

"Try telling him you're leaving."

"What if he says, 'Go ahead and leave'?"

Will-John put both elbows on the table and

regarded Bonnie soberly. "Try it anyway," he said quietly. "You don't have to leave. Just *tell* him you're leaving. That might get him married to you quicker than you think."

"I wonder," Bonnie said dubiously.

"Hell, put up a For Sale sign in your front window. He can't help but see it when he comes here. Advertise it in the *Banner* so everybody knows it. If anybody offers to buy it, turn 'em down. Just make Cole think it's going to happen."

"Well, nothing else has worked," Bonnie said, and shrugged her shoulders. "Why not try it?"

From the front of the house came the sound of a knock on the door, insistent and loud.

A voice called, "Let me in, Bonnie. I know you're there."

Will-John stood up, picked up his hat, said, "Let him in, Bonnie, and good luck." He kissed her and she willingly kissed him back, pressing her body against his. Then he moved to the back door. As he stepped out into the alley, he heard Cole's continued knocking.

Walking down the alley, he remembered how long and carefully he and Bonnie had worked on this during the past six months that they had known each other, and how perfectly it had shaped up. . . .

At last fall's beef delivery he'd met her in

Kansas City, where she was waiting on tables in the dining room of the big hotel where he was staying. The day before he had delivered a trainload of Burt Hethridge's Triangle H beef, received an enormous check which he immediately deposited in a bank for transfer home, then went out on the town with the paid-off crew.

They'd caroused until daylight, when Will-John, drunk enough, had pulled away from them and headed for his hotel suite. He'd drowned in sleep for almost the whole day and wakened at evening. He bathed and shaved and afterwards dressed in a dark suit and white shirt from the suitcase he had stowed in the stock train's caboose at the loading.

Looking at himself in the mirror, he decided he was clean enough and handsome enough and big enough to attract any woman, and tonight he meant to do just that.

The big dining room downstairs was only half full, for it was late. The headwaiter, a dandified Italian, led him to a table for two against the mirrored side wall, seated him, then turned and snapped his fingers for a waitress.

What the signal brought was a small grey-uniformed young woman of startling beauty — blue-eyed, black-haired, and full-bosomed. It took him less than three minutes to find out her name was Bonnie Leal and to ask her advice on the menu. She suggested sea food, which she guessed he hadn't had for a while, so he started out with oysters and a dark beer. She was solicitous, pleasant, laughed at his jokes and his stories about the other times he had stayed here after disposing of Triangle H beef. All the time she was busy, refilling his glass, hotting up his coffee, bringing fresh rolls and more butter, and when she served him she managed to brush his shoulder with a soft breast, an act which was not unintentional, Will-John knew.

With his dark good looks, his curly hair, his obvious virility, his almost raffish humor, Will-John was used to attracting women. He prided himself on being something of a womanizer, but this girl was hard to pigeonhole. Behind her friendly manner was something indefinable. By brushing her breasts and hips against him, was she trying to tease a big tip out of him, or was it something else again?

When he had finished his roast duck and she was transferring his plates to the tray, he asked idly, "Doing anything tonight, Bonnie? I'm alone on the town except for my crew. They've seen enough of me and I've seen enough of them."

"I'm not doing anything, but where'll we go?"

Will-John smiled. "Not where I usually go. You name it."

"Well, there's a minstrel show in town. Is that too tame?" She looked at him with those wide eyes, mischief lurking in their grey depths.

"Not if we have a couple of drinks first."

"I won't go in a saloon."

"But you'll have a drink?"

"Why, of course."

"What about my room?"

Bonnie nodded. "As long as the door's open."

Will-John laughed. "I'll be waiting."

She filled his coffee cup, picked up the tray and headed for the kitchen.

When she brought him his dessert and check, she said, "Fifteen minutes."

Will-John nodded. "Room eighteen."

He wolfed down his dessert, moved out into the lobby, where he paid for his dinner, and then told the porter to fetch a bottle of good whiskey and two glasses to room eighteen.

In his two-room suite upstairs, he left the door open and waited impatiently for the whiskey and even more impatiently for Bonnie.

As he paced the parlor of the suite, he wondered what the night would bring. After last night's carousing, much of it with the dance-hall girls, the edge was off his woman hunger. Still, Bonnie was a pretty girl whom he had had no trouble in picking up.

Bonnie arrived along with the porter and the whiskey, glasses, ice and water. She had changed from her uniform into a navy cotton dress edged with white lace, and her small white straw hat made her hair seem even darker.

Will-John paid the porter, who left, and then he asked Bonnie to sit down. She chose a seat on the sofa against the wall and chattered about the coming minstrel show while he mixed the drinks on the half-moon table between the room's two windows.

When he had brought her drink and sat down beside her, she moved toward him so that her thigh touched his.

Will-John had known many women, so many of them that he knew that some wanted to touch and be touched. These women seemed to draw from bodily contact the warmth that animated them. Bonnie, he guessed, was one of them.

"You alone here in town, Bonnie?" he asked.

"Yes. I live here on the top floor with another girl who's a maid. Why?"

"I noticed the wedding ring."

"Oh, that." She held up her left hand and looked at the gold band. "It's kind of handy when a drummer or a cowboy gets fresh."

"Then it's not a real wedding ring?"

Bonnie gave him a crooked smile. "I'm afraid it is."

"Then where's your husband?"

She shrugged. "He was soldiering in the East. When I heard he was being transferred to the West, I married him to get West."

"All right. But where is he?"

"I wouldn't know. I left him two years ago in St. Louis."

"Hasn't he tried to find you?"

Bonnie took a sip of her drink, and laughed quietly. "No. No more than I've tried to find him. It wasn't what you'd call a marriage really. He wanted someone to sleep with and cook for him. I wanted to get out of a family of ten and away from a drunk father that wanted me to go on the streets." She shrugged again. "When we both got what we wanted that was the end of it. When he was transferred again to Indian country, I said that wasn't for me. We parted friendly enough."

This was a strange enough story, Will-John thought, but at least the girl was honest. Obviously she liked men and, just as obviously, men would like her, for she was young and had an animal attractiveness.

He asked, "What if you want to get married again, Bonnie? What if I fell in love with you tonight? We couldn't get married, because you've already talked too much."

Bonnie looked at him coolly. "What if I've been lying to you?"

Will-John took a sip of his drink and said thoughtfully, "I don't think you have."

A wise amusement came into Bonnie's eyes. "Well, are you in love with me? Do you want to marry me?"

"What if I said yes?"

"Well, I'd say I'd been lying and there's no way you could prove I wasn't."

Will-John laughed. This girl had lived by her wits and he had a feeling she was still living by them.

"Are *you* married?" Bonnie asked.

Will-John rose. "No, and not about to be. Bonnie, what about our minstrel show?"

Bonnie drank the last of her whiskey and stood up too.

Down on the street, Bonnie told him that the theatre was only a block and a half away and that they needn't bother hiring one of the hacks that hung around the hotel's entrance.

As they started out, Bonnie took his arm and pressed against him, and again Will-John was reminded of her need to touch and be touched.

The theatre was less than half full. There were, he noted, many women and children in the audience. In a community made up mostly of men who liked their pleasures as rough as possible, he guessed there was very little entertainment fit for women and children.

The minstrel show bored him, but he was amused at the simple pleasure Bonnie seemed to get out of it. If the story of her life was only partly true, he guessed her pleasures had been small and seldom, and that this singing and joking might hold a huge appeal to her.

His thoughts strayed then and they returned, as always, to Triangle H. Burt Hethridge, sick as he was, would be cheered by the size of the check from the Commission House for their beef. It would go, of course, into making Triangle H even richer, so that whoever married Sarah and Cole could live like a king and a queen.

But Sarah, he figured, would probably wind up an old maid. There wasn't a man in this crude West who was good enough for her, in her own view. Cole, on the other hand, liked women and they liked him. The trouble was the women he liked impressed by his name and his money, and they were easy women. As a consequence, Cole had very little respect for the opposite sex. Will-John could not imagine what sort of woman would eventually catch him and his money. She would have to be beautiful, fun-loving, informal, and not overly educated. She would have to be tolerant of his weaknesses, which were many, and of the wild streak in him.

He was brought back to the present by Bonnie's laughter at the clowning on stage. She snuggled her shoulder against his, as if unconsciously inviting him to put his arm around her, and again her thigh, warm and soft, pressed his. He looked at her, and in the half darkness she was any man's dream of a happy and beautiful girl.

It was then, at that theatre on that night, Bonnie beside him, that the idea came to him. It came with a slow stir of excitement. When he had considered it, a vast impatience came to him. He was still reviewing what he was going to say when the program came to an end amid applause.

Bonnie chattered about the show on the way back to the hotel and Will-John listened impatiently.

When they came to the lobby, Will-John said, "Come up to the room for a nightcap, Bonnie. I've got something I want to talk over with you."

Bonnie looked at him curiously and said, "All right, but just one, Will-John."

In the parlor of his suite, Bonnie took her former seat on the sofa. If she noticed that Will-John had closed the door, she made no mention of it. Will-John mixed their drinks, gave Bonnie hers, and then, instead of sitting beside her, he drew up an armchair facing her. He took out a cigar from the breast pocket of his coat, lighted it, and then began by saying, "You told me a lot about yourself tonight, but you haven't asked me anything about myself. What do you know about me?"

"I asked about you from Charlie. He's at the desk. He said you deposited one of the biggest checks the bank had ever seen."

"Only a small part of that was mine, Bonnie. The rest goes to a sick old man and his son and daughter."

"Lucky them," Bonnie said.

Will-John went on to describe Triangle H's vast holdings, and as he talked Bonnie's eyes widened. Then he told her of Burt Hethridge and his heart condition, which would continue to worsen until his death in the near future. He explained that all the Hethridge holdings would be divided between Sarah, a prim twenty-two-year-old, and Cole, who although he was only twenty-four was a talented hell-raiser. He drank and gambled and chased women, all of whom thought he was a charmer.

When he paused to relight his cigar, which

41

had gone out as he talked, Bonnie said, "This Sarah — has she got a beau?"

Will-John said no, and Bonnie asked, "What's the matter with *you?* You could put up with any woman for that much money." Bonnie's eyes were bright with excitement or greed, and maybe both, Will-John was pleased to observe.

"I'm ahead of you, Bonnie. I've proposed a dozen times and it's still no."

"Has Cole got a girl?"

Will-John said quietly, "No, but she could be you, Bonnie."

Bonnie sat utterly still, looking at Will-John with a wild disbelief in her eyes. Then she let out the breath she had been holding. "What a tease you are, Will-John."

Will-John, leaning forward, elbows on knees, said, "Not tonight I'm not, Bonnie. Answer me some questions now, and tell the truth. Are you married?"

"Yes."

"That won't make any difference. Throw the ring away and you're not married. Is Leal your married name?"

"No, my born name. My married name was Carpenter — Mrs. Jethro Carpenter."

"Now think carefully, Bonnie. You're a waitress in a hotel. What else can you do?"

"What else?"

"Yes. I reckon you haven't got much schooling, so you wouldn't know figures."

"I'm a good cook if I've got something decent to do with."

"What else?"

Bonnie said promptly, "Well, I made this dress. Do you like it?"

Will-John said he did, and then he went on. "Where did you make it? How did you make it?" he demanded.

"Almost my first job was cutting and sewing in a factory. We made uniforms, and after hours dresses. I still make dresses after hours."

"Who for, and where?"

"Why, in my room, and for the dance-hall and sporting girls. I do some work for Madam Marie when she gets orders for things she doesn't know how to make. I make her hats too."

She paused and said half angrily, "What is this?"

Will-John smiled. "We've got it Bonnie. Just answer me one more thing. Why do you do it?"

"Why, to make money. What else? I get room, board and tips here. Anything else I want, I have to earn the money to buy it. Besides, what's all this got to do with what you were talking about?"

"Everything, Bonnie. If you were a hotel

waitress, Cole would go for you like he does for all the others. But not if you were the owner of a dressmaking shop."

"With what money?" Bonnie asked wryly.

"Mine."

Now Bonnie's eyes came really alert, and Will-John continued talking. She would come to Pitkin in two months' time, he said. Between now and then she would have bought materials and all the foofaraw that goes into women's clothes and hats. She would set up her dressmaking shop in town and, inevitably, she would get business. It didn't matter how little or how much. She would establish herself as a young woman in distressed circumstances. Just as surely Cole would meet her, since just as, for certain, women could speculate and gossip about her. She could catch Cole any way she chose, but the fact of her public respectability had to be established.

Bonnie listened eagerly, nodding when Will-John said she could catch Cole in any way she chose; she only smiled wisely.

When Will-John had answered most of her questions, she came to the big one. "What I don't understand, Will-John, is what you get out of this. Do you want me to pay you?"

"Here's what I get out of it, Bonnie. We've got a range war coming to a head out there. There'll be shooting. In six months after

44

you're married to Cole, you'll be a widow."

"How do you know that?"

Will-John said quietly, "I'll see to it."

Bonnie's eyes widened. "You mean you'll kill him?"

"No, but he'll be dead. That I promise you." He paused and smiled. "Another thing I promise you, Bonnie. After a proper length of time you'll become Mrs. Will-John Seton."

Bonnie looked stunned. "You'll marry me, you're saying?"

Will-John nodded. "It'll be a marriage just like your first one, Bonnie. Both of us want something. I want Triangle H, and you want money and security. Together we'll own half of Triangle H through you."

This was coming faster than she could comprehend it. Again Will-John saw the calculation in her eyes and he knew he had made the right choice. He asked, "What are you thinking about, Bonnie?"

"I — I just don't know what to think."

"I'll tell you one thing you'd better not think about. Don't think about getting the money and running out on me without marrying me. If you try it, I'll find your Jethro Carpenter through Army Records. They'll prove you were married when you married Cole Hethridge. Any court would rule you have no claim on Cole's estate, since you weren't legally married to him. Do you follow all that, Bonnie?"

"I follow it, but why would I run out on you?"

"You ran out on one husband, remember."

Bonnie flushed. "That was different. He was dirt poor and so was I. This time you won't be dirt poor and neither will I."

"Good. Just so you remember it."

"Won't Sarah be trouble?"

"No, because I keep the books," Will-John said. "They'll show that we're being rustled to death by the nesters that already hate us. Tallies will go down. Hands will be laid off. We'll be borrowing and things will look bad. That's when I point out to Sarah she had better get a more secure place for her money than a ranch that's in trouble. We dicker, and I buy her out with the money that's been loaned us with our half of the Triangle H for collateral. We'll own Triangle H ourselves. Our loan'll be paid back immediately by the sale of what we call our Number Two ranch. We'll still have one of the biggest ranches in the state."

"My God!" Bonnie whispered, and again Will-John saw the avarice in those beautiful guileful eyes.

"How does it sound?" Will-John asked.

"Why, like it would work."

"Then you'll do it?"

46

"Wouldn't I be crazy if I didn't."

Will-John said mildly, "Yes, you would."

That was the way the pact had been made. Up to now it had worked just as planned. Burt Hethridge had died, Cole and Sarah had inherited Triangle H, and Cole was wildly infatuated with Bonnie. Except, as of today, he had avoided making good on his promise to marry her.

4

Cole had his hands cupped on either side of his temples to screen out the light so he could look through the half-glassed door into Bonnie Leal's shop. With his right foot he kept kicking the base of the door, raising a thunderous racket. It hadn't brought him success before and he didn't think it would today.

Suddenly he stopped the kicking, for the draperies parted that curtained the corridor leading back to the dressing room, Bonnie's bedroom and the kitchen. Bonnie appeared, and made her way past a pair of dressmaker's dummies in front of the shelved bolt goods, skirted the cutting table, came up to the door and unbolted it.

The sight of her moving through the room, and the wild hope that she would see him had a sobering effect on Cole, so that when she opened the door he was steady on his feet as he gave her a mock bow.

Bonnie said coolly, "Why do you have to

make that racket, Cole? The whole town can hear you."

"Let me in and I'll be quiet. Don't, and I'll keep it up."

Bonnie gave him a resigned smile. "All right, come in."

Cole managed not to weave or stumble as he stepped past Bonnie into the cutting room and made for one of the straight-back chairs at the cutting table.

"I think you'd better sit down," Bonnie said dryly.

"I do too," Cole said, and he pulled out a chair and sank into it. The room was not pin-wheeling and he saw only one of Bonnie, so he knew he was reasonably sober. She circled behind him and took the chair across from him.

"Make it short, Cole. What do you want?"

"Why, I want it like it used to be, Bonnie," Cole said sulkily. "Why are you doing this to me?"

"You damn well know why I am," Bonnie said shortly. "We're through. Can't you get that through your head?"

Cole looked at her morosely, and remembering, said, "We can't be, not after what we've been to each other."

"We can be, are, and will be," Bonnie said flatly. She stood up. "You stay there, and I'll bring some coffee."

49

"I'll come back with you."

"No, you won't," Bonnie said firmly. "You'll sit right there or you'll leave."

Cole had started to rise, but now he sat back and watched Bonnie going out of the room, her back straight, her hips swinging in a way that brought the cruelest of memories to him. He remembered that day three months ago, when his sister Sarah, who learned he had business in Pitkin, asked him if he'd bring back a dress from Bonnie Leal's dressmaking shop. He didn't know Bonnie Leal or know of her shop, since that was women's stuff. He found the shop tucked away in a side street, and she was, he learned later, new to Pitkin and was being tested by the ladies of the county who lacked the taste or the time or the ability to dress themselves attractively. At first sight of her he was stunned by her beauty, and he wondered why he and others had not heard of her. He asked her.

"I only work with women and I'm too busy to go out. I work here, eat here and sleep here, so what man would see me?"

"I'll fix that." He asked her if he could take her to the social and dance at the Crossley Crossing school that Saturday night, and she consented. By the time the evening was over he knew he was in love with her and already jealous of the attention men were suddenly

50

paying her. For the next five nights he drove into Pitkin after dark with the red-wheeled buggy and they drove around the night-deserted country roads. On that fifth night, holding her in his arms, he told her he was in love with her and she confessed she was in love with him.

He had learned by then that she was affectionate and liked to be kissed and fondled, but only up to a point. He knew he had found a girl who would not wholly give herself to him, and this not only hurt his pride and vanity, but made her even more desirable. Within another week he had proposed they become engaged to be married. This ruse had worked with other hard-to-get girls, who, once they had his promise, would give themselves to him. Bonnie agreed to the engagement, but her relations with him were different afterwards from what they had been before. She was pushing him to set a date for the marriage when Burt Hethridge died.

His father's death, a month and a half ago, interrupted their meetings only briefly, but afterwards Bonnie had changed. She had pushed him even more insistently to name the date of their marriage.

Cole was caught between two selfishnesses. One was that he knew he would inherit money which would free him to do anything he

51

wished. He could travel, gamble and buy women. The other was that he could have Bonnie by marrying her, and thus end his torment. By nature indecisive, he kept postponing his decision. He told Bonnie the court had put him on a small allowance until the estate was settled, not enough for them to live on. When she offered financial help, he said his pride would not allow him to accept it. When his inheritance was clear, he said, they would be married and could move to Triangle H.

It was then that Bonnie gave her ultimatum: she would no longer see him. True to her word, for the last ten days she had kept her doors locked against him. He retaliated in the only way he knew how, by seeking out other women, by drinking too much and by gambling recklessly. None of it succeeded in blanking out the memory of Bonnie.

At this moment he was still surprised that she had permitted him to see her, and he came to his decision.

Bonnie came sideways through the draperies, a cup of coffee in each hand, and moved towards him. Even in this shapeless work smock, she seemed beautiful and infinitely desirable. She set his cup of coffee before him and then sat down across from him.

"That should sober you up enough so you won't fall down when you leave." She added,

"That will be very shortly."

Cole could only look at her, feeling that old wild hunger for her, wanting to take her in his arms and knowing that he couldn't — yet.

He took a sip of the scalding coffee and didn't even taste it. Putting down the cup, he said, "Know what day tomorrow is, Bonnie?"

"Why, Thursday."

"A Thursday you'll remember, because it'll be your wedding day."

The shock of surprise reflected on Bonnie's face was genuine, but it was only momentary. She said with quiet bitterness, "You're drunk."

"A little," Cole conceded. "But I know what I'm saying."

"Yes, but will you remember it?"

Cole smiled. "If I don't, you remind me."

Bonnie looked at him searchingly for a long moment, studying his handsome, haggard, drink-flushed face. She said, "If you're serious, Cole, you can prove it."

"By marrying you now?" Cole stood up. "Come on, let's go to the courthouse."

Bonnie rose too. "Oh, no. You'll never be able to say I caught you drunk and married you." She walked over to him and put her arm through his and said, "Come with me."

She guided him across the cluttered room, and he was weaving on his feet. Parting the curtain, she led him into the dimly lit corridor and steered him to her bedroom. Here she halted and steadied him. Moving over to the bed, she removed the spread and turned down the blanket and sheet. Then she turned back to him and said, "Can you get your boots off without help?"

Cole said thickly, "What is this, Bonnie?"

"You're going to bed, Cole. When you've had a night's sleep and I've fed you breakfast, then say what you said a couple of minutes ago." She paused, faced him and put her hands on his arms. "Or don't say it."

She moved close to him, pressed her body against his and kissed him, and before he could raise his arms to encircle her, she stepped back out of reach. Without another word she went out into the corridor, drew the curtain across the bedroom entrance and was gone.

Back in the kitchen she stood still, listening. Had she been a fool not to take him up on his offer to marry her now? After all, whether he was drunk or sober when he married her, she would still be his wife. But no, she didn't think she'd made a mistake. If he was sober when he married her, nobody, not even Cole, could accuse her of taking advantage of his drunken condition.

And he would marry her, Bonnie thought with sly certainty. If he went to sleep, it would be with the memory of that soft body

54

he coveted against his own.

When she heard the creak of bed springs, her breathing returned to normal, and she smiled to no one but herself.

When Will-John Seton turned out of Bonnie's alley onto the side street, he halted and took out a slip of paper from his shirt pocket. It was a list that Sarah Hethridge and the cook had given him. As he checked it to make sure all items had been attended to earlier, his dark, weather-browned face held a faint smile of derision. He realized only too well the absurdity of Triangle H's thirty-year-old foreman, boss of forty men, owner of a herd of his own, the absolute law on thousands upon thousands of acres of grazing land, shopping for items wanted by a twenty-two-year-old girl and a Mexican cook. It was a chore for the lowliest ranch hand, but he had taken it upon himself in order to spend an hour plotting strategy with Bonnie. He discovered as he balled up the shopping list and dropped it in the street that he was thirsty, and he headed for the main street.

Will-John was not an over-tall man but his chest was deep and his shoulders wide and heavy. His broad face with its high-bridged Roman nose held a kind of reserve that went properly with authority. Below his full-lipped mouth there was a deep cleft in his chin. He

55

was dressed in clean range clothes, and a worn shell belt and holster sagged at his right hip. When he reached River Street, instead of turning left toward the River House, which had the best bar in town, he turned right and headed for the First Chance, the saloon patronized by the hard-scrabble nesters and small ranchers, the poor and the broke.

On every visit to Pitkin Will-John made it a point to have a drink at the First Chance. It was small, dirty and shabby, and here the hard-pressed, two-bit ranchers grumbled at the weather, drank mostly beer and gambled for peanuts. But beyond that, they were obsessed with a not-so-quiet hatred of the role Triangle H had played and was playing in their fortunes. They were suffered to exist in the big ranch's shadow, and that knowledge galled them to a man. They consistently stole Triangle H beef. As long as they killed to feed their families, Will-John didn't bother them, but if they stole beef in quantity and attempted to drive it out of the country, they were caught and whipped, and their sorry cabins were burned down. Those who resisted were hunted out of the country by Triangle H hands. Formerly Burt Hethridge, and now Will-John, never deigned to haul them into court. Triangle H enforced its own laws.

Each visit to the First Chance, Will-John

knew, was a fresh throwing down of the gauntlet, as it was intended to be, the continuing show of Triangle H's power and contempt for those who hated it.

Will-John passed the feed stable, noted that his loaded buckboard was still in the runway, and paused there long enough to tell the hostler to hitch up the team. Afterwards, he continued down the street past the blacksmith's and came to the First Chance.

On either side of the shabby frame saloon were vacant lots, as if nobody wanted to have it as a near neighbor. Half a dozen saddle horses and a buckboard were tied in the shade of the cottonwoods across River Street.

Will-John shouldered through the batwings, then halted just inside and to the left of the door to let the gloom of the place soften the sun glare in his eyes. As he was waiting, he heard the desultory talk of some men at the bar trail off and cease. When his eyes had adjusted to the semidarkness, he saw that the rearmost of the two gambling tables had a card game going. The five men playing were looking at him, just as were the bar customers. The bar was on the right and ran the length of the narrow room. As Will-John walked up to it, he nodded to the room without speaking, and when he reached the bar he said, "Hot day, Tim," to the bartender.

Tim O'Guy, who owned the saloon, was a gross, balding Irishman of fifty with pale, chill eyes that never held a warm welcome for anybody. He moved tiredly toward Will-John, rubbing his open hands down his thighs over a filthy, stained, once-white apron.

"You've come to the right place to cool off, Will-John. Beer like always?"

"That's it. See what the rest of the boys'll have. If it's too hot to drink, give 'em a cigar, Tim."

Will-John turned to face the room and put both elbows on the bar, hooked his boot heels over the bar rail and leaned back. This was the moment he looked forward to on each of his visits. Some men would not accept a drink from the Triangle H foreman, but they would silently accept a cigar. If there was anyone hardy enough to refuse both the drink and the cigar, there was a good chance of trouble. Now Will-John looked at each man individually. He identified everyone except one of the card players seated in a chair against the wall. This was a tall rangy man who Will-John guessed was a Texan. His bleached eyes were proud-surly and the stare he gave Will-John was overlong and held an unmistakable dislike.

Will-John heard Tim put down his glass of beer on the bar behind him, and waited as

Tim drew beers first for the men at the bar and then for those at the table. For perhaps the hundredth time, Will-John regretted that Tim O'Guy had never been able to afford a back bar mirror, not even a cracked one with half the silver gone. The lack of it forced Will-John to look at the room to see who refused his drink, or who refused both drink and cigar. With a back bar mirror, he could have caught it without seeming to stare like a schoolteacher watching for whispering or spit-ball throwing.

When Tim reached the Texan, the Texan shook his head. Tim reached up into the upper pocket of his buttonless vest and drew out a cigar which he laid beside the Texan's arm. The Texan, looking at Will-John, picked up the cigar and tucked it back in Tim's vest, still looking at Will-John.

Lazily Will-John turned, picked up his beer, as did the other men, lifting their glasses in surly acknowledgment. Will-John took a deep draught of the almost warm beer and then, beer glass in hand, moved over to watch the card game. He halted behind the player who was facing the Texan. There were two raises to the Texan, who doubled the last raise. In turn around the table each man threw in his hand. The Texan showed his openers and threw the rest of his hand face down on the pile. There was some soft swearing, even some laughing from the other players, but the Texan raked in the dirty chips unsmilingly.

One man said, "We got a rough customer here."

Will-John said quietly on the heel of the man's words, "That's because he's pure, Davey. He doesn't drink or smoke, because they dull the mind."

This, of course, was intended as an insult, just as the Texan's refusal to accept the drink or even to pocket the cigar had been intended as an insult.

The Texan looked up from his pot and said quietly, "Yeah, I'm pure — purely mean."

The man in front of Will-John slid sideways out of his chair and the other three were not slow to follow.

Will-John had been careful to drink his beer with his left hand, leaving his right hand free. Now he said, half-smiling, "Show me, Texas."

The Texan's eyes seemed to go flat; he started to rise as Will-John moved strongly and swiftly to put his thighs against the table and drive into the Texan, shoving him still half-seated in his chair against the wall. The Texan sat down and rode his chair helplessly. When his back was pinned against the wall, Will-John with his right hand gave the round table a quarter-turn which moved it a little off-center to the Texan's right, pinning his gun hand and gun into a tight pocket and foiling any attempt at a quick draw. Will-John set down his beer and moved to his right so that the Texan could not shoot his legs under the table. Will-John drew his gun now.

His weight still pinning the table against the Texan, Will-John called, "Bring over a beer, Tim."

The whole room watched. Tim drew a beer and came over beside Will-John with it.

"Put it in front of Texas," Will-John said.

Tim reached the beer across the table and set it in front of the Texan.

"Leave your right hand where it is, Texas. Drink that beer with your left."

The Texan, murder in his pale eyes, only shook his head from side to side.

Will-John, still keeping pressure on the table, came around it and with a swift, rough movement, yanked the Texan's hat off. He set it brim-up on the table, poured the glass of beer into the crown then picked the hat up and clapped it on the Texan's head. The beer cascaded down into the Texan's eyes and over his face, and now Will-John, gun held hip-high, took the pressure off the table and backed away.

"Something eating you, Texas?" Will-John asked.

"It'll keep," the Texan said softly, wickedly. He lifted both arms, shoved the table away from him, took off his hat and let the remainder of the beer drench his face and shirt. Will-John holstered his gun and walked slowly down the bar, reached in the left pants pocket of his levis, took out a coin, put it on the bar, said, "See you sometime, Tim."

Then, his back to the Texan and the others, he started unhurriedly for the batwing doors.

"Stop right there, Seton!" An iron voice called.

I should have backed out, Will-John thought dismally. Then he thought with pure fear, *Not in the back,* and slowly he turned and saw Texas, gun drawn, skirt the table and move slowly toward the bar, never taking his eyes from Will-John. Texas halted at the bar and said, "A pint of whiskey, Tim, and pour it all in a glass."

O'Guy reached under the bar, brought out a pint of whiskey, reached down again and brought out a water tumbler. Uncorking the bottle, he filled the glass and set it alongside the Texan.

Will-John looked over the room and felt a grey knowledge of defeat. The odds were too high to take a chance on going for his gun.

Texas took the glass in his left hand and slowly approached. He halted just out of reach of Will-John and with a fast lift of his left arm he shot the glass full of whiskey at Will-John's face.

Will-John saw it coming and tried to turn his head but, he was too late. The whiskey caught him on the cheek and splashed into his eyes. Instinctively, he brought both hands up to wipe the stinging whiskey out of his eyes, and even as he did so he heard the shouts of laughter in the room. He rubbed his smarting eyes and then opened them. The room was out of focus and blurred by the whiskey mixed with his tears. Blinking, he waited until the room came into focus. Texas, his shirt drenched, his face still beaded with drops of beer, put the empty glass on the bar and then said softly, "Now you can go."

"Where can I find you, Texas?" Will-John asked.

"Don't bother. I'll find you."

Will-John nodded, turned and pushed through the batwing doors to the street. The fury he felt almost choked him. As he turned up toward the feed stable, his eyes still smarting, his anger gave way to a raging sense of humiliation. He, and therefore Triangle H, had been challenged. Even if Texas was only a hard-case drifter passing through, the harm had been done, and every nester in that saloon would rue this day they had laughed at him.

At the feed stable he tramped down the runway, passing his team and buckboard. At the water trough at the corral behind the stable he took off his hat, hung it on a post and doused his head in the water of the trough. Afterwards he wiped his face on his shirt tail, put on his hat and went back to the buckboard and climbed onto the seat.

As he pulled out into the street, he looked down at the First Chance. *You don't know it, Texas, but you're dead,* he thought; and thinking it, he felt a curious relief. As he reviewed what had happened, one thing stood out. When he had asked Texas where he could find him, Texas had replied, "Don't bother. I'll find you." That meant Texas would be around and that was comforting; he would make an example of him that those nesters would never forget. Thinking that, he dismissed the whole thing from his mind.

5

Thursday, press day for the *Pitkin Banner*, was a busy day for Rich Sturdivant and his devil, Billy Arnold, but for Kate Canaday it was almost a day of rest. While the shop turned out the paper, Jeff Bagley, the blond hobbledehoy of a young man who drummed up ads and was a reporter too, took care of the out-of-town mailing list. Kate was as idle as she wanted to be. For her the week's work was done. The week's edition, good or bad, was out of her hands.

By custom, everybody came to work early on press day, Kate included. After her father's death, once she had the *Banner* running smoothly, she thought it would be nice to sleep on press day, since she wasn't needed, but habit conquered. To lie abed in the tiny house beyond the courthouse while the fruit of the week's labor was being harvested four blocks away seemed almost sinful, certainly irresponsible. So this morning, before daylight, she had dressed, breakfasted and walked through the wonderfully cool dawn past the court-house to oversee her crew in the shop.

By seven o'clock, when the stores opened and traffic began, Kate was finished billing her advertisers. She rather looked forward to the rest of the morning when she would per-sonally hand-deliver bills to her advertisers, gossip with them, listen to their praise or complaints, acquire news items and put a friendly gloss on their business relationship. Accordingly, she had dressed more carefully than on working days, and this morning she was wearing one of Bonnie Leal's creations, a light cotton print dress of a green that matched her eyes and was cleverly designed to mold her figure while demurely revealing it. It was new and was intended for Sunday church, but it had been irresistible today. That it was a success was confirmed by the smiles of appreciation from the man and two boys in the shop when she came in. Her tiny hat that hugged her sleek hair was as saucy as the person who made it, again Bonnie Leal.

Kate collected her bills, stepped out into the newly awakened morning and began her rounds. Her third call was at the big red brick county courthouse where she would present a sizable bill for the county's legal advertising in the *Banner*. The brick walk that led from the street to the courthouse was tree-shaded and so cool that some of the bricks held a bright green moss in their joinings. Her destination was the county clerk's office, which because it was the most used of all the offices, was the corner room, first door to the right of the long corridor.

A big brick vault took up perhaps a quarter of the large, high-ceilinged room. A long counter barred public access to it, and between this counter and the vault there were desks for the county clerk and his deputy. When Kate walked in Matt Wittman, the white-haired clerk, was seated at his desk calling a list of numbers to his deputy inside the vault. He ceased his chanting at sight of her and said, "Morning, Kate," rising and limping toward the counter.

On his way he said appreciatively, "Lordie, that's a pretty dress!"

"Thank you, Matt," Kate said. "You wouldn't have said that if you'd seen the bill I'm leaving you."

Matt Wittman's white mustaches lifted at the corners as he smiled. "I've been expecting it, and so have the commissioners."

Kate took the bill from her purse and laid it on the counter. Matt didn't look at it but looked at her instead.

"You're the second pretty girl I've seen this morning. Today's my lucky day."

"Who was the other?"

"Why, Bonnie Leal. She come in with young Hethridge to get a marriage license. Or I guess it's the other way around. He come in with her."

A look of mild surprise touched Kate's face and she said, "Poor girl."

The old county clerk looked carefully at her, wondering if he should say what was on his mind. He did. "I wouldn't say poor, would you?"

Kate laughed quietly. "I didn't mean that, Matt. Still, it would take an awful lot of money to make a real husband out of him — more than's been minted."

"Well, maybe she'll straighten him out."

"Then we should wish her a long life. She'll need it for the job."

Now Matt looked at her bill and said, "I'll give this to the commissioners at their Monday meeting, Kate. Is that soon enough?"

"Of course. Good-bye, Matt." She started for the door, then halted and turned. "Matt, did they say when they were going to be married?"

"Well, he asked me if Judge Conover still had his rooms at the River House. That sounds as if they were going there from here, doesn't it?"

"Yes, it does. . . . Good-bye again."

Out on the walk, Kate pondered old Matt's news. She had no special feelings about this sudden marriage. Cole's wild ways, she guessed, or rather hoped, could be curbed by Bonnie's sweetness and her down-to-earth practicality. Just how Sarah Hethridge would receive this news Kate could guess. She would hate her brother's wife living in the same house with her, and inevitably there would be a conflict of rights. That is, if Cole and Bonnie planned to live at Triangle H.

At the end of the brick walk, she halted, opened her purse and leafed through the remaining envelopes containing bills. When she came to the bill for James Donovan's legal notices, she grimaced and started to put it aside in her purse to give to Billy Arnold for delivery. Up until Donovan's visit yesterday they had used boys off the street as vehicles for communication with each other. But now Kate held the Donovan bill in her hand and felt an inner push of malice. Did Jim Donovan know of Cole Hethridge's marriage yet? She doubted it. Then why not deliver his bill and give him the news, which was sure to unsettle him.

Her mind made up, she set out for Donovan's office on River Street, but now she felt a little ashamed of the motive behind her visit. But his tongue-lashing yesterday was intended to humiliate her, and had. It was, she felt, reasonable enough to fight back.

The Stockman's Bank on the corner faced River Street, and on the side street there was a railed stairway leading to the second story. On its half-glassed door, visible from both River Street and the side street, was painted in white letters JAMES DONOVAN, ATTORNEY AT LAW, and below it, D. HEATH, SURVEYOR.

Kate climbed the stairs now and opened the door that led into the short cross corridor that divided the second story in half. On the right was the door into the surveyor's office; on the left was the door, now open, which led into a small reception room that held half a dozen chairs and a bare table directly under an overhead kerosene lamp. Beyond this room was Jim Donovan's office. Its door was open and Kate moved around the table, halted at the door and knocked.

"Come in." Jim Donovan's voice sounded surly, as if he had spotted her approach and was primed for something disagreeable.

Kate stepped into the carpeted office and noted that the bookshelves on the right were in more of a mess than when she had been here last, which was some months ago. They held books and papers jammed together in Donovan's own private, untidy filing system.

Then she saw Jim seated at his desk. It was placed crosswise to the corner so that he could, seated in the swivel chair behind it, look at the room and out the windows at River Street and the cross street.

A look of surprise came into Donovan's face now, but watching himself, he rose and said without any enthusiasm, "Good morning, Kate."

"Morning, Jim." She reached in her purse and drew out the bill, then stepped forward and put it on the corner of his desk. "It's payday, sort of."

Kate noticed first that he had this morning's issue of the *Banner* open on his desk, and then, raising her glance, she surprised him watching her.

"You're sort of dressed up for a newspaper editor, Kate." Donovan observed. "Most of them I've ever known sleep in their clothes and wash their hands in printer's ink."

Kate smiled faintly. She regarded his townsman's coat, white shirt and black string tie before she observed, "You're sort of dressed up, too, for a cowman. Most of them I know look as if they sleep in their clothes and don't even wash their hands."

This retort brought a smile from Donovan, and he shook his head. "You know, Kate, you fight back even before there's really anything to fight about. All I was trying to say was that that's a pretty dress and it becomes you. Now can we sit down and pick a subject we won't scrap over — if there is one."

Kate settled herself into the armchair facing the desk and Jim sat down after she was seated.

"Well, there's always the weather, Jim, but maybe we won't have to talk about it. I've got a little item that should interest you."

"A news item?"

"Very much so," Kate said. "Am I the first to tell you that Cole Hethridge and Bonnie Leal took out a marriage license this morning and asked directions to Judge Conover's rooms? Old Matt was guessing that they'd ask the judge to marry them. Maybe they're even married now."

Jim Donovan couldn't entirely hide the look of surprise, almost consternation, that washed over his lean face. He was silent for a moment, watching her, and then he said, "You wouldn't be getting even with me for yesterday, would you Kate?"

"A little," Kate conceded. "Anyhow, it's true. Does it bother you?"

Jim frowned. "Its suddenness does." He paused and thought a moment. "This marriage should have called for a big wedding out at Triangle H. A hundred people from all over the state, and certainly the Governor. You know, a boxcar full of champagne, a half-dozen barbecued steers and a trip to Europe for the bride and groom." He grimaced. "If Burt Hethridge were alive, that's what it would have been."

"You mean it seems a little furtive?"

"Good word. Yes, I do. Know any reason for it, Kate?"

"Well, there's always the classic one, isn't there?'

"But do they see each other? I never see them together." He scowled. "Oh, maybe once or twice, but I've seen Cole with other girls more than with her."

"I don't think I've ever seen them together," Kate said. "Still, I'm a stay-at-home mostly, so I'm no judge."

Jim turned his head and looked out the window at the big cottonwoods across the street and Kate studied his profile. When he wasn't mad, as when she had last seen him, his face was an odd mixture of an esthetic outdoorsman and tough saloon brawler. Each of course contradicted the other, but there it was.

"What do you know about this Bonnie Leal, Kate?"

"Only that she's very pretty, very bright, and the best dressmaker and milliner I ever ran across."

Jim looked appraisingly at her and said, "If that's a sample you're wearing, I agree with the last. But where did she come from?"

"Nobody seems to know," Kate said slowly. "She was poor and has worked to save up money for this shop, is all I know." She paused. "Does it matter?"

"Only to Cole, I reckon," Jim said. "I'm meeting with him at eleven o'clock. There'll be two other gentlemen meeting with us. I expect that as executor, I'll be writing out checks to these gentlemen in the sum of about seventy-odd thousand dollars. Tomorrow I'll report to the court that the estate is free of encumbrances. The new Mrs. Hethridge will have married herself into a quarter of all the Triangle H holdings." He added dryly, "It'll bring in a little more money than her dressmaking job does."

Kate nodded, smiling appreciatively. "Jim, when you see Cole today, ask him where they're going to live — at the home ranch with Sarah, or at another of their places."

"For the *Banner?*"

"Why in the world not?" Kate asked almost sharply. "Haven't you ever read a newspaper story of a wedding? They all end with something that runs like this: quote, the newly married couple will return to the new home awaiting them in Barber's Itch, Missouri, unquote."

Jim Donovan laughed and, as far as Kate could recall, it was the first time she had heard him laugh aloud.

"All right, I will." Jim said. "But can't you ask?"

"Not him nor Sarah. They took the same view of what I wrote about their father that you did. They'd tell me to go to hell. Sarah would call it hades."

They heard the sound of footsteps in the corridor and then in the reception room.

"That will be Cole," Jim said. "I told him to come a little early."

Kate rose now and said, "Don't forget to tell me where they'll live, Jim."

Jim nodded and came round the desk and walked with her to the office door. She said good-bye and moved into the reception room. Cole was standing on one side of a long narrow table, and when he saw Kate he looked away. Kate chose the other side of the table for her exit and didn't even look at Cole as she went out.

"Come in, Cole," Jim said.

Cole was still wearing the ruffled shirt and red vest with gold buttons, and as he came past Jim he trailed a cloud of alcohol.

Jim closed the door and then said quietly, "I understand congratulations are in order," and put out his hand.

They shook hands briefly and Cole asked, "Then she told you?"

"She just came from the courthouse, so the word's out."

"Well, let it be," Cole said cheerfully.

Jim moved over behind the desk and gestured to the chair facing it that Kate had just vacated. Cole sat down and Jim sank into his swivel chair.

"I was going to talk about your debts, Cole, but that was before I knew you were married."

"What difference does that make?" Cole asked, bridling.

"Not any. Tell me about this marriage."

"Well, for one thing it's legal. I've got Judge Conover's certificate in my pocket if you don't believe it."

"Oh, I believe it. I just wondered how it happened with no warning."

"Because we felt like it," Cole said in surly defiance.

"Been planning it long, you two?"

"Since before my father died."

"Did he and Sarah know you'd planned it?"

"What is this?" Cole said angrily. "I don't have to answer to you or anybody else."

"Were you drunk?" Jim persisted.

"It happened about an hour and a half ago. Do I look drunk? What the hell's the matter, Jim?"

"Nothing's the matter. I'm just curious. For the past two months I've been handling an estate that's one of the biggest ever probated in the state. Now a girl I scarcely know will share your half of it. Does she know what it's worth?"

"How could she, when I don't even know? You said even you didn't know."

"You been seeing much of her, Cole? If you have, why haven't we seen you courting?"

Cole flushed, whether in anger or embarrassment Jim could not tell.

"We had a fight and yesterday we made up, but all along we figured on getting married."

"Where did you see her so often?"

"At her place, damn it! It was our business and not the town's." He leaned forward. "What are you trying to do, Jim?"

"Only understand."

"Well, you can't stop or change it now it's done."

"Granted, but what do you know about your wife?" Jim asked quietly. "Have you met her parents? Do you know where she comes from? Do you know who her friends are? Matter of fact, what do you know about her except she's very pretty?"

Cole said hotly, "Her parents are dead! She's worked since she was a young girl. She learned the dressmaking business and supported herself."

"Where?"

"Kansas City and other places. I don't know where else, and I don't care. But I do know what you're asking is none of your damn business. Keep it up and I'll — " He didn't finish.

"You'll what?" Jim asked.

"Just get off my back," Cole said angrily.

"I'm not on your back. I've been your lawyer. People are going to ask me about this quick marriage."

"Tell them to wait nine months and see how wrong they were."

Jim pushed now. "And about the girl you married?"

Cole rose out of his chair, took a step and put both clenched hands on Jim's desk. "Tell them any damn thing you want, Jim. But if you foul-mouth her I'll kill you."

"Why should I foul-mouth her?" Jim asked quietly. "I don't know enough about her to, and I wouldn't if I did. I'm just trying to understand why the way everybody else gets married wasn't good enough for you or for her."

Cole stood up and said bitterly, "Give it up, Jim. We're not ordinary people. I've always been a maverick, as you should know."

The sound of men's voices in the reception

78

room came to them both and Jim rose. "And as you are about to demonstrate," he said drily. "Let's go out and face the music."

Jim went across the room, and into the reception room. Two men there who had been conversing now stopped their talk: Case Harvey, the big hulking owner of the River House, was talking with Tom Dunning, owner of the Cameo Saloon. Tom was a small, soft-voiced man in a black townsman's suit, so diminutive that Harvey had to drop his thick shoulders and head to hear him.

As Jim walked toward them he said easily, "Morning, gentlemen. When money's waiting, we are always prompt, aren't we?"

Case Harvey's heavy, flushed middle-aged face, pitted long ago by smallpox, broke into a smile as he extended his hand.

"Our last chance, isn't it?" Tom Dunning murmured.

Jim shook hands with him too. "That's right, Tom. Tomorrow, I account to the court." He turned and gestured to Cole, who had halted at the end of the table. "Gentlemen, I think congratulations are in order. Cole is a brand new bridegroom this morning."

Harvey and Dunning looked at each other in mild surprise.

"Congratulations, Cole," Harvey said gruffly. "Who's the bride?"

"Case, you wouldn't know her unless you wore a dress and a feathered hat. It's Bonnie Leal, the dressmaker. She's Mrs. Cole Hethridge as of an hour and a half ago."

Both Dunning and Harvey came forward, shook hands and congratulated him. Cole accepted their congratulations with a reserve that told them he knew the enemy in spite of all the polite words.

It was Jim who broke the awkward silence. "Why don't we sit out here? It'll be cooler too if we get down to shirtsleeves." He pulled off his coat, as did Dunning and Harvey. Before Harvey threw his on one of the straight-back chairs against the wall, he took out a crumpled wad of paper which he placed on the table. They sat down then, Cole and Jim side by side facing Harvey and Dunning across the narrow table. Dunning was wearing red sleeve garters which Jim suspected he had filched from one of the girls at the Cameo.

"Well, let's get started on what we're here for. I assume you two gentlemen have read this morning's *Banner* and my notice to creditors. At least, if you haven't read it, I sent you a message."

Case Harvey raked his meaty fingers through his pale, sparse straight hair and yawned. "Yeah, I got your message and I read the notice." He reached out and swept the several pieces of crumpled paper in front of Jim. "I'm a creditor to the tune of forty-eight thousand dollars. These are Cole's I O U's to me. Want to add them up, Jim?"

Jim rose. "Let me get some paper and a pencil." As he went into his office, Cole reached out and began to examine individually the I O U's. When Jim returned Cole said sharply, "I won't honor that. That's not my handwriting."

Before Harvey could answer, Jim said, "Let me handle this, Cole. First, let's add them up." He sat down and looked at Dunning. You've got some too, Tom, haven't you?"

Dunning nodded, and with lazy precision reached in his trouser pocket and brought out a roll of papers tied by a silk thread. When he broke the thread the sheaf of papers slowly expanded. He put it in front of Jim.

Jim began on Case Harvey's pile and found that Case was right in his calculation. He put Harvey's slips aside and began on Dunning's neat pile. "I make it thirty-eight thousand, five hundred. Correct?" Dunning nodded.

Then Jim returned his attention to Harvey's pile. As he began to go through the papers he said, "Cole, look at each one and tell me if that's your signature. See if you can remember signing each one.

"Ha!" Harvey's snort of derision held the

deepest measure of contempt. "They're dated, Jim, but if you find any two signatures alike, I'll eat your hat." He looked at Cole. "And if you can remember signing them, I'll eat yours too."

Cole flushed and began to look at the I O U's one by one as Jim passed them to him.

"That's not my signature," Cole said, holding out one the slips.

Case Harvey reached out, took the slip, glanced at it and threw it on the table. Then he leaned back in his chair. "That's one of your left-handed ones, Cole. You used to think it was funny to sign left-handed. Or maybe it was because you had a glass in your right hand and couldn't be bothered to put it down."

Cole eyed him with hatred and returned to his examination. When Jim had handed him the last one and he glanced at it, he put it aside, making a separate pile of four slips he had rejected. He picked them up, handed them back to Jim and said, "I never signed these. Somebody else did. Your houseman maybe, Case."

Jim looked at the four slips, did a swift mental calculation, then raised his glance to Case Harvey, whose face was getting redder by the minute. "These come to thirteen thousand, Case. The signatures are barely readable."

"If you were halfway into your second quart, yours would be too, Jim," Case retorted. His voice had suddenly gone gravelly with the effort to suppress his anger.

Jim set them aside and reached again for Dunning's pile. He and Cole went through the same procedure as before, and Cole isolated three from this group. It was pretty much the same story; the signatures were illegible, and when Jim added up Cole's rejects, they came to three thousand, and he told Dunning so.

Tom nodded impassively and said, "So altogether, out of eighty-six thousand five hundred, you won't honor sixteen thousand."

"Did I say that?" Jim asked softly.

"I did," Cole said flatly.

Dunning's sallow face was impassive. "All right, I'll accept your welsh on my three thousand, Cole. Just don't come near the Cameo again."

Case Harvey looked at Dunning with an expression of disbelief. "You're letting him welsh?" he asked. At Dunning's nod, Harvey crashed his clenched fist onto the table top. "Well, by God, I'm not!" he said. "That thirteen thousand is money owed, and I want it." He rose, putting both hands on the table, and stared furiously at Cole.

Jim said, "Easy, Case."

Tom Dunning slipped out of his chair, moved over to his coat and put it on.

Cole Hethridge, staring into Case Harvey's meaty face, felt a reckless anger. He had triumphed over Dunning and he aimed to triumph over Harvey. He was about to speak when Tom Dunning's soft voice said, "I'll take my check now, Jim."

Jim nodded and rose and turned his back on that frozen tableau — Case Harvey leaning over the table staring furiously at Cole Hethridge; Cole, with sullen triumph in his eyes, returning the stare, and Tom Dunning standing aside. As Jim turned into his office and headed for the desk, he heard Cole say, "No, Case, not ever."

Jim was seated at his desk and was pulling the checkbook from the top drawer when he heard a chair scrape and tip over. He heard Cole's strangled, "No, no," and then Jim moved swiftly. He leaped from his chair and was around the desk and through the doorway. As the reception room came into his line of vision, he saw what had happened. Case Harvey had vaulted over the table, seized Cole by his shirt front and yanked him out of his chair.

Jim moved through the door just as Harvey drove a shoulder-heaving blow into Cole's jaw. Cole's head swiveled sharply, his knees sagged, but Case held him upright, Cole's head lolling back. The second blow was even more savage, and Cole, head back, was utterly vulnerable. Harvey got that blow in at the exposed throat and jaw before Jim was on his back, trying to pin his arms. Cole slumped to the floor, unconscious, and Case kicked out at his head, driving a boot into Cole's cheek.

Jim wheeled Harvey around, and it took enormous effort to move him in a semicircle away from Cole.

"Cut it out, Case!" Jim said sharply. Harvey wrestled a futile five seconds and then Jim felt the slab of muscle across his back relax, along with the arms, and he freed him. Walking around him, Jim looked down at the unconscious Cole. "Leave him alone, Case. You won't get your money from a dead man. Now stay set while I get Tom's check."

Jim went into the office, and wrote out a check to Tom Dunning for thirty-five thousand five hundred dollars. When he came back to the reception room, Dunning was still standing in the corner, and Harvey, hands in his hip pockets, was looking out of the window. Cole lay where he had fallen, blood oozing from the cut on his check. Jim stepped over him and handed Tom the check. Dunning thanked him and left, and then Jim moved over to Case.

85

"Cooled off enough to talk sense, Case?"

Case turned his head and looked at him. "Try me."

"All right. Without that thirteen thousand that Cole questioned you've got a pile of money."

"Thirteen thousand is a pile of money," Case growled.

"But easy money, Case, taken from a drunk kid."

"Are you saying my game is crooked?"

"I'm not even hinting it. I'm just saying you should do what Tom Dunning did. He knew there was a risk in taking that amount of I O U's from Cole. So did you. Tom felt he was lucky to collect the biggest part of it. So should you."

"Well, I'm not," Case said flatly.

"All right, let's take it to the Judge."

Case snorted. "You know damn well there's no legal way to collect a gambling debt."

"I didn't mean I'm going to take it to law, Case. Let's show the Judge those signatures along with the others. See if he thinks they should be honored."

"Ah! I know what he'll do," Harvey said disgustedly. "He'll tell you not to honor any of them."

"Got a better idea, Case? As you say, we don't have to honor any of them, but we are

86

honoring most of them."

Harvey turned his huge head and stared broodingly over the town. He heaved a deep sigh and said, "You've got me, Jim. Better something than nothing."

Jim snorted in derision. "Pretty tidy something, isn't it? Without the notes in dispute, I make it thirty-five thousand. Will you take a check for that?"

Harvey hesitated, and then said, "I'll take it but I'll figure a way to get the rest of it."

"Better make it a safe way, Case."

Jim went into his office and made out a check to Case Harvey for thirty-five thousand dollars, returned to the reception room and gave Harvey the check.

Accepting it, Case said flatly, "Like Tom, I don't want to see that whelp in my place again. Tell him." He took his coat from the chair, threw it over his arm and tramped out.

Afterwards, Jim came around the table and knelt by Cole. Rolling him on his back, Jim felt his pulse. It was slow but even, as was his breathing. He turned back one of Cole's eyelids and passed a hand across his line of vision. There was no reaction. He felt Cole's jaw, moving it from side to side, and satisfied himself that it was not broken.

What do I do with him? Jim wondered. Then it came to him that the rear of Bonnie

Leal's dressmaking shop opened onto the alley across the street. Now that Cole had a wife, let her take care of her husband, he thought sourly. He stood up and put on his coat, got his hat from the office, closed and locked the office door, and then came over and straddled Cole. Reaching down, he heaved Cole to his feet, ducked his shoulder and let Cole tumble forward over it.

6

Minutes later Bonnie Hethridge opened her kitchen door in answer to Jim's knock. Her blue eyes widened at sight of Jim's burden.

"Mrs. Hethridge," Jim began, "I wish you every happiness with this package I've got over my shoulder. Where would you like me to put him?"

"Is he drunk?"

"Just unconscious. From a beating Case Harvey gave him."

"Bring him in," Bonnie said resignedly. Jim followed her across the kitchen, noting her trim figure in the rose-colored silk dress. She had a cloth tape measure around her neck, and Jim wondered if even on her wedding day she was at work. In the corridor Bonnie held the curtain back and Jim moved into her bedroom and eased Cole onto the patchwork bedspread. He loosened Cole's string tie while Bonnie drew off his shiny half-boots. Then, standing side by side, they regarded Cole.

"Should I call the doctor?" Bonnie asked.

"If he doesn't come around pretty soon, I would."

"Let's go where we can talk," she said. She led the way back to the kitchen, gestured to the round kitchen table, and moved over to the cupboard and took down two cups. After she had filled them with coffee from the pot on the stove, she came back to the table, put down Jim's cup beside his hat and moved the sugar bowl toward him. Then she sat down across the table from him.

"He said he owed Case Harvey money. Tell me about it."

Briefly Jim told her of the disputed I O U's and of Harvey's demand that they be paid, and of the fight that took place while he was out of the room to get Dunning his check. Bonnie listened carefully, and Jim was quietly surprised at the calmness of this girl. *She's known trouble before,* he thought, and said, "Mrs. Hethridge, Coles's debts are all paid up now — all seventy thousand dollars of them. If he hasn't learned his lesson this trip, he'll be owning another seventy thousand in six months."

"No, he won't" Bonnie said firmly. "Things are different now."

"I hope you're right." Jim took a sip of his coffee and looked around the clean and tidy kitchen. "Do you plan to stay here, Mrs. Hethridge?"

Bonnie smiled faintly. "That name is so new, I keep wanting to look behind me for a Mrs. Hethridge. Why don't you make it Bonnie?" At Jim's smile, she said, "We won't live here. But I'm going to keep the shop. Maybe come in a couple of days a week by appointment."

"You'll live at Triangle H?"

"Yes. Cole wants to."

"You know Sarah, of course?"

Bonnie nodded and smiled. "I know what you're thinking, Jim, but I can get along with anybody."

"Does Sarah know you two are married?"

"By the time we get out there I expect she will," Bonnie replied quietly. "I don't think she'll like it either."

"For what reason?" Jim asked curiously.

Bonnie shrugged, almost with indifference. "Did you ever know a sister who thought any woman was good enough for her brother to marry?"

Jim smiled. "Come to think of it, I haven't." He paused. "I'm going to ask you a question that's none of my business. Don't answer if you don't want to." He saw a fleeting alarm in those blue eyes, and then it was gone before Bonnie said good-humoredly, "Ask it, and

91

I'll judge if it's any of your business."

"All right. Most girls want a big fuss made over their wedding. New clothes, rooms full of presents, a big reception, lots of champagne and every relative that can be rounded up. You settled for a simple ceremony. I'll bet Judge Conover had to call in the housekeeper to be a witness. Cole would have caved in if you'd asked him for a big wedding. Why didn't you?" He saw the flush mount in Bonnie's cheeks and wondered if his question had embarrassed her, or if it had angered her.

"Why, it's simple enough," Bonnie said. "I've no family. I've been on my own since I was sixteen. Cole doesn't give a hoot about his relatives and I don't give a damn about being paraded before them. Also, I think Cole was afraid of Sarah. There's nothing she can do now except sulk. This morning was the way we both wanted it." She finished proudly. "It was just right."

Jim was silent a moment regarding her, and she held his gaze unwaveringly.

"You sound as if you are defending yourself."

"And you sound as if you are accusing me."

"Of what?" Jim said quickly.

Bonnie made a swift impatient gesture with her hand as if she were brushing crumbs off the table.

"Of not being a starry-eyed young girl and not doing what is expected of me and not caring if a preacher blesses this marriage." Her eyes were cold and her voice was hard and determined. She said, "Cole doesn't give a damn about what people think of him, and he never has. I don't either. Is that enough of an answer?"

"More than enough," Jim said, and then on impulse he asked, "Why are you mad, Bonnie?"

His question surprised her, Jim saw, and he watched her as she swiftly seemed to collect her thoughts and discipline them for speaking.

Bonnie said, "Up till today I didn't know you except to say hello on the street. The only reason I've said what I have is that you're Cole's lawyer. That doesn't give you the right to talk to me like a psalm-singing preacher. Now I've told you all I'm going to."

"I don't think you have," Jim said quietly.

Bonnie was silent a moment and her eyes held a wariness. "I suppose you're right. From now on, every time I open my mouth in front of you I'll give away something about myself. That's what you think, isn't it?"

"Yes," Jim said. "And every time I open my mouth in front of you I give away something about me. That's a fair trade, isn't it?"

"Yes, if we're friends."

"Bonnie, we're not enemies." Jim said patiently. "How can I help you? You're going to the ranch today?"

"If Cole's up to it."

Jim said with seeming irrelevance, "Got any new dress goods in, Bonnie?"

"Why, yes. Why?"

"Then snip off a couple of samples for Sarah to look at."

"Do you think that will buy off her anger?" Bonnie asked, contempt in her voice.

"Oh, no," Jim said. "It'll show her that you and Cole expect her to accept this marriage as natural. To prove it, you're doing what is natural. You have some new dress material you think she'd like, and since you're going to see her you brought some samples along. Does that make sense to you?"

Bonnie gave him a crooked and meager smile, and slowly got up from her chair, not looking at him. She said, as is to herself, "You think like a woman." Then she added, "No, that's not right. I'm a woman, and I would never have thought of that. Maybe you just think like a lawyer."

"That's what Cole pays me to do, Bonnie." He rose. "Thanks for the coffee, and take care of our boy."

"From now on," Bonnie said quietly.

Once in the alley, Jim turned left, heading for the *Banner* and Kate. As he walked in the hot midday sun his conversation with Bonnie kept teasing him. *Hot and cold, thick and thin, sad and merry, wild and tame, they are all opposites and only opposites can describe that girl.*

He passed the River House and he was tempted to stop by for a drink, which, considering the morning he had spent, was called for. But more than he wanted a drink, he wanted to talk with Kate.

The doors of the *Banner* were open, inviting the breeze from the river. As he entered he saw Kate seated at her desk beyond the counter and he moved through the swing gate as she looked up at the sound of his footsteps.

She had taken off her hat and was wearing the ink-stained apron that he had come to think of as her working uniform. Back in the shop Rich Sturdivant, the press run finished, was working at the job press. Its clamor filled the whole building with a clattering racket. Again, tomboy fashion, Kate put two fingers in her mouth and delivered a shrill whistle. Rich heard it and stopped the press, and Kate called, "Go out and get a beer, Rich. We want to talk."

Without a word, Rich stepped out of the open back door and vanished. Kate retrieved her hat and purse from the chair alongside the desk and Jim sat down.

"Something's happened," Kate said.

"Does it show in my face?"

"You were seen carrying Cole over to Bonnie's. The *Banner* never sleeps, you know."

"I told you it was payday for Cole's gambling debts."

"I know, but what happened up in your office?"

Jim told her of the disputed notes Harvey held, and of Harvey's attack on Cole. He finished up saying, "I couldn't stay there all day holding his hand, so I took him back to Bonnie."

"That's a nice present for a wedding morning," Kate said reflectively. "How did she take it?"

"Almost as if she expected it," Jim said, frowning. "No, that's not quite right. She took it in stride, as they say. No alarm, no crying, and mighty few questions."

"Did you ask her where they're going to live?"

"Yes. At Triangle H with Sarah, because Cole wants it."

"Do you think *she* does, Jim?"

Jim tilted back his head and rubbed the side of his face with the palm of his hand. "I don't know, Kate. This Bonnie puzzles me."

He went on to tell her of his conversation with Bonnie, which, now that he put it fairly in words, made Bonnie sound as prickly as a porcupine.

When he had finished Kate said, "She sounds as if she had a mind of her own."

Jim nodded; then he said slowly, "She's hiding something, Kate." After he said it he wondered why he had.

Kate looked at him with open curiosity. "Be specific."

"Well, when I asked her if I might ask a question which was none of my business it scared her."

"What was your question?"

"Pretty trivial — why she didn't hold out for a big wedding like the average girl. The point is, she was scared before I asked the question. Why?"

Kate thought a moment and then said, "That's really a hell of a way to put anything to anybody, Jim. In the first place, when you asked if you could ask a question that's none of your business you as good as warned her it was going to be unpleasant, didn't you? I'd be a little wary myself."

"All right, so I put it clumsily," Jim said. "Still I had the feeling she was afraid of what I was going to ask."

Kate smiled, "Like, 'Are you a fortune-hunting hussy, Mrs. Hethridge?' "

"Exactly."

Kate shook her head. "Jim, is there a person alive who hasn't done something he's ashamed of? When you asked Bonnie your clumsy question she was trying to defend some secret. Who wouldn't? I would, and you would." She paused. "I don't think you're being fair to her."

"Maybe, but it's just a feeling I can't shake."

"What was her answer when you asked about the quick marriage?"

Jim told her, and added, "In effect she told me if I didn't like it I could lump it, which is fair enough."

"Has Sarah heard about the marriage, or doesn't Bonnie know?"

"Bonnie couldn't tell."

Kate leaned back in her chair, clasped her hands on the back of her neck and looked up at the ceiling. Jim had the feeling that if he hadn't been there she would have swung her feet up on the desk.

"Why don't you beat them out there with the news, Jim?"

Jim showed his surprise. "Why, it's none of my business, Kate."

"You're Cole's lawyer, and Sarah's too. Whose business is it if it isn't yours?"

"What would it accomplish to tell Sarah they're married?"

"For a while she's going to feel as if a mule's kicked her. At least that much would be out of the way before she sees them."

Jim scowled. "I don't get that mule part, Kate. Why would Sarah feel that way?"

Kate snorted. "Haven't you read any of those female English novelists? They would say that Cole 'married beneath his station.'"

"But Sarah's not a female English novelist. Her own mother married a hard-drinking, hell-raising Texas cowboy. She was a schoolteacher, so he was beneath her station."

"How little you know her," Kate said, almost with derision. "Sarah isn't a product of either of her parents. She's a product of an Eastern finishing school. They made her into a stiff little snob. Do I have to tell you that?"

"I guess you do, so tell me."

Kate unclasped her hands and put them on the desk. "Do any of the nice young men in town try to court her? No, they're scared to death of her. She makes them ashamed of what they do and what they are. Have you ever seen her at a dance? Oh no, that's country stuff held in the schoolhouse or the Masonic Hall. A ballroom and orchestra is what Sarah wants, with all her dancing partners wearing white ties and claw-hammer coats."

485771
T/35L

"How do you know all this?" Jim demanded.

"Why, I've got eyes and ears. But go ahead, you describe her to me."

"A shy, sensible, high-minded girl."

"If that's true, that should make your visit out there all the more necessary to break the news to this shy little girl. But be sure to tell me how she reacts to it will you?"

"But I haven't said I'm going."

"Well, are you?"

Jim groaned, "All right damn it. I'll go." He rose. "I'll feel like a fool, Kate."

"You shouldn't. You're paid to look out for her. It would seem awfully strange to her if you didn't think it was worth bothering with."

"Trying to make a substitute uncle out of me?" Jim asked sourly.

"That's what you are, isn't it? The family lawyer?"

"Not after tomorrow when I turn in my executor's account to the court."

"Nonsense!" Kate said crisply. "The next scrape Cole gets into he'll head for you. The first problem Sarah has about the ranch she'll head for you too." She smiled. "Now, on your way, Uncle Jim."

On his way back to the livery stable, Jim pondered his conversation with Kate. She had maneuvered him into doing something he didn't want to do, but underlying her prodding was plain common sense. It was true that both Cole and Sarah considered him their family lawyer. Each year after the sale of the Triangle H beef, he was consulted about investing the money. Outside of a few contributions to Eastern charities out of Sarah's portion, Jim always advised them to invest in breeding stock, to put back the money Triangle H earned them into the ranch. Kate was right in another way too. In the end, all of the ranch's legal problems would be laid in his lap.

At the livery stable he inquired if Cole had left town. The hostler checked and said his horse was still in the corral. Jim asked that his own bay gelding be saddled, and when it was ready he tested the cinch, mounted and rode out of town.

He was immediately on Triangle H range, and if he chose to keep riding twenty-five miles he would still be on it. As a matter of record, the townsite of Pitkin had been Triangle H range and it was deeded over by Burt Hethridge. Four miles south and perhaps half a mile west of Pitkin, Triangle H headquarters was snugged into the piñon-and-cedar-stippled foothills of the Longbows that towered to the west. When he was still a mile from it, he could see the lighter green of the cottonwoods that flanked Alder Creek, which passed thirty yards from the main house on its way to join the Cheat farther east.

7

Once the road reached Alder Creek and followed its course, the whole big spread suddenly came into view, mirrored in the lake that had been made by damming the creek below the house. The big bunkhouse and cook shack were built of weathered logs, as were the barn, the wagon shed and the blacksmith's shop. Beyond them were the corrals abutting the big horse pasture. An addition to the bunkhouse of lighter colored logs had been built when Burt Hethridge became ill and this was the office from which Will-John Seton managed the ranch affairs. These buildings were clustered well away from the main house, and were surrounded by huge cottonwoods.

The two-story house was a frame affair, and anything but plain. There was gingerbread on the eaves and above the windows that overlooked the lake, and on the front porch that faced it. The kitchen wing was built of logs and was the original humble ranch house. On the other side of the Big House was a one-story frame bedroom wing. Everything that wasn't whitewashed log was painted white.

Jim had always been puzzled by the hugeness of the house, with its many rooms. It was as if Burt Hethridge had built it to house ten children and their children. Even the white picket fence enclosing a huge lawn seemed designed to protect children from falling in the lake. The fence started at the corner of the porch, ran down to the lake shore, turned and went to the tumbling creek, and then came back to join the bedroom wing.

At the tie rail by the office Jim dismounted. As he was tying his horse, Will-John Seton came to the office doorway. "How are you, Counselor?" he called.

Jim moved around the tie rail and came over to him. "Scared, Will-John. Is Sarah at the house?"

"I reckon so, but why are you scared of her?" There was a look of amusement on the foreman's face as he added, "I think you could lick her, if that's what you had in mind."

"I might have to," Jim said quietly. "You see, Cole got married this morning to Bonnie Leal."

A look of incredulity spread over Will-John's handsome face and he murmured, "Well, I'll be damned. Are you sure?"

Jim nodded. "I wanted to break the news to Sarah before they get here."

"Well, break it then. There's nothing she can do to change it is there?"

"Well, she could scold him to death," Jim said dryly.

"She's tried that already and it didn't work," Will-John said, then added as if to himself, "Cole married! So, maybe that'll straighten him out."

"Well, I'd better open the ball." Jim turned and headed for the house and Will-John watched him. He was smiling, and there was a look of purest pleasure on his face. His wildest hopes had come true, and he hadn't even known about it.

Jim went through the gate, mounted the porch steps, crossed the porch and twisted the bell handle in the middle of the half-glassed door. It clanged with a loudness that was startling. He supposed it was designed to sound in the farthest reaches of the house. After waiting a moment, he extended his hand to ring again when the door opened suddenly and he was looking at Sarah Hethridge.

She was a tall girl, slender rather than thin. She was wearing a man's shirt with the sleeves rolled up and a tan divided riding skirt. Her faintly sunken cheeks made her brown eyes seem enormous; her chestnut hair was tied at the back and curled down over her left shoulder. Her mouth, unlike Cole's pouty one, was wide and thin-lipped. "Come in, Jim," she said. "I saw you ride up."

She stepped aside and Jim took off his hat and moved into the parlor. It was a pleasant and familiar room to him, and he could remember a younger, gawky Sarah sitting at the flat writing desk under the side window. In a quick glance around the room he guessed he had interrupted her writing now.

She gestured towards the horsehair sofa and Jim moved across the room wondering how to open this.

"I thought this was one of your days in town, Jim."

She moved across the rug, swung the chair out from the desk, and Jim sat on the sofa. His uneasy hands held his hat between his knees. "All my business was done, Sarah, except for my visit out here."

"Oh? What business do you have here?"

"No business," Jim said wryly. "I just came to tell you something, Sarah."

"Is Cole hurt?" Sarah asked quickly.

"Not hurt. Married. To Bonnie Leal. This morning, early."

Sarah sat for a stunned moment, her mouth open, then she came swiftly to her feet. "That's not true, Jim! You're teasing me!"

106

"I've got Cole's and Bonnie's word for it, and that's something you can't lie about."

Jim noticed that the color had drained from Sarah's face and that her hands were clenched at her sides.

"Bonnie Leal!" Sarah said with a furious contempt. "Why, she's trash!"

Jim said nothing, and Sarah started to pace the floor. She passed him and made a half-circle, and when Jim looked at her her eyes were blazing with anger. "She can't do it, Jim! Was Cole drunk?"

"If he had been, Judge Conover wouldn't have married them."

"But she's nothing — she's nobody!"

"Pleasant enough, isn't she?"

"Yes, when she's selling you dress goods," Sarah said. She took up her pacing again but then stopped abruptly.

"Jim, can this be annulled?"

"On what grounds?"

"Cole's sick from drinking. He didn't know what he was doing."

"No sicker than he's been for three or four years. No, Cole's of age. He knew what he was doing."

"But that woman!" Sarah said shrilly. "She doesn't even know Cole. She's after his money, and nothing else. She's a cheap, common fortune-hunter, that's what she is!"

"Sarah, Sarah," Jim said quietly. "All you really know about her is that she's attractive and a clever dressmaker. Why don't you wait to learn more about her? Anything else is guessing, and you know it."

"Oh, that silly idiot Cole! I could kill him!" A sudden thought came to her. "Where are they going to live?"

"Here."

"Oh, no," Sarah said warningly. "They will *not* live here."

"Everything your father left is half Cole's, Sarah. That includes this house you're standing in."

"I know that, but the house is always the woman's, even if the law doesn't say so."

"You could read that to mean his woman's, Sarah — Bonnie's."

"No! I won't live under the same roof with that woman."

"Not even try to?"

"No, you'll have to arrange something, Jim. Give Cole a piece of my share of the land in exchange for the house. Why" — she looked about her as if she were seeing this room for the first time — "this is all I have. This is my life. Do you think I'm going to share it with a stranger?"

Then Jim saw her face alter; she was looking past him through the window above the desk. Jim turned his head and through the window saw Cole and Bonnie seated in a buckboard halted in front of the office. Will-John Seton, hat in hand, was talking to them, and Jim noted the big trunk in the bed of the buckboard which undoubtedly held Bonnie's clothes and other possessions. Even as Jim and Sarah watched, Will-John put on his hat and started toward the house. Cole swung the team in behind him.

Jim stood up and said, "Be kind to her, Sarah, if only for Cole's sake."

He started for the door, but Sarah said in a panic, "You're not going, Jim?"

"I've done what I came to do."

"No, no, you can't go!" she cried. "Nothing is settled. You've got to back me up, Jim."

"Back you up? How?"

Sarah clasped her hands together in silent anguish, shook her head and wailed, "I don't know, but you've got to help me."

In the silence that followed they could hear the gate creak, and then the sound of footsteps on the porch.

Sarah seemed frozen. She stood still, and turned only when she heard the door open. In silence they watched Cole, carrying Bonnie in his arms, cross over the threshold. Both of them were laughing as Cole set her down.

He looked at Sarah and Jim and gave a mock courtly bow, his arm across his middle as he said, "Sister mine, this is my wife."

"So I've just been told," Sarah said coldly.

It was Bonnie that Jim was watching. He saw her quickly size up Sarah's reaction to the marriage, and her present temper. Bonnie said easily, "Hello, Sarah."

Sarah looked at her as if she were offal, then her chill glance shifted to Cole. "It must have been a beautiful wedding," she said sardonically. "Bridesmaids, flower girls, organ music and a big reception. Was it like that Cole?"

Cole's face flushed under the lash of her temper and he said sullenly, "Quit it, Sarah. It doesn't matter how we got married. We are just married, and we did it the way we wanted."

"The way you wanted, or the way she wanted?" Sarah asked.

In her grey, long-sleeved dress trimmed with narrow red braid, Bonnie stood almost defiantly straight. "The way he wanted. His wishes have always come first with me."

"How God-damned sweet!" Sarah said bitingly.

Her profanity shocked them all, and it was a measure of her reckless anger.

Cole retorted, "Keep your foul mouth shut, Sis." He took a step toward her and said,

"This is a fine, warm greeting, I must say."

"It's what the occasion deserves."

They all heard the commotion outside as Will-John wrestled the trunk up onto the porch.

"If those are your wife's things they can stay right out there."

"Oh, can they?" Cole said in a flat voice. "This is half my house, Sis."

"It's my house!" Sarah said. "All you do is eat here once in a while and sleep here."

"Are you trying to tell me that Bonnie and I won't live here?"

"Ask your wife if she wants to stay where she's not welcome."

"I don't have to," Cole countered swiftly. "This is my home and she's my wife."

Jim was studying Bonnie for some clue as to her feelings. He knew it was humiliating for her on her marriage day to be discussed as if she were a piece of unwanted livestock, but if she felt it her face didn't show it. She seemed interested, even amused, at this outrageous reception.

Sarah turned to Jim now and said, "Jim, you be the judge. Do I have to put up with a strange women in my house?"

Jim said dryly, "What if you brought a husband home, Sarah? Would Cole have to put up with him?"

Cole gave a bark of a laugh. "Anything she brought home I wouldn't have to put up with, Jim. I'd leave."

Sarah was watching Jim as if he had slapped her. He pushed his point. "Was that a fair question, Sarah?"

"Yes, and it gives me an idea."

Sarah crossed the room and called through the dining room toward the kitchen, "Ceferina, will you come here, please?"

They all waited in silence until a broad-beamed, pleasant faced, middle-aged Mexican woman dressed in black stepped into the room.

"Ceferina, I want my trunks packed right now. I'll lay what I want packed on the bed."

She walked into the adjoining library and then they heard her climbing the stairs. It was Jim who said, "Ceferina, this is Señor Cole's brand-new Señora."

As Bonnie crossed the room Ceferina curtsied, then shyly accepted the hand Bonnie held out to her. While the two women spoke briefly, Jim reached for his hat and moved towards the door. "See you later, Sport."

Will-John was muscling the trunk across the porch, and as Jim passed him he said, "The groom is just inside, Will-John, get him to help you."

Walking out of the shade of the cottonwoods into the bright hot sunlight towards his horse, he was thinking that if he hadn't heard Cole and Bonnie's welcome by Sarah he would never have believed it had happened. The whole thing was appallingly ugly, and he remembered, wincing inwardly, his description of Sarah to Kate — "a shy, sensible, high-minded girl." Kate had been right about Sarah, a stiff snob of a girl, but how could this have escaped him for so long? He supposed that Sarah's distant friendliness to him was just another facet of that snobbery. Because he had an education in law, she would treat him as an equal — but all non-equals, beware!

Untying his horse and stepping into the saddle, he could not help but wonder where Sarah would go. Abruptly it came to him that he was fed to the teeth with Burt Hethridge's two children. Cole had proved himself a welcher, and he himself had abetted him. He wasn't ashamed of bargaining for a client with a couple of gamblers, but it left a bad taste in his mouth. Sarah had shown herself to be a selfish harridan. *Then let them go their separate ways,* he thought grimly as he rode out past the lake, forded Alder Creek and struck out south across the foothills for his own D Cross.

8

In another hour he was on his own range, and as he rode through it he eyed it critically. The spring had been a good one, with more than enough grass to carry his stuff until the snow line receded in the Longbows and the calves could travel. The summer rain would help it further, but the fact was that if he hadn't had the new lease for summer graze in the Longbows to take the pressure off, he wouldn't have had enough graze for the coming winter. If a man had luck with his increase, there was a natural reaction. Either he had to acquire new range for the increase, or keep his count at the same old level that the range would sustain. Sometime soon he thought he should try to make a deal with Will-John Seton to lease a chunk of Triangle H grass that surrounded him on three sides.

Just before dark he came in sight of D Cross. It lay at the wide mouth of a timbered canyon. Wherever there was water in this country there were cottonwoods, and that was the case here. A big spring up the canyon surfaced just long enough to supply D Cross with water, and then went underground again, its run so short it had never been dignified by being named a creek. The shallow run of water, perhaps eight feet wide, divided the three-room log house from the small log bunkhouse, the wagon shed and the corral opening onto the horse pasture.

As he approached in the dusk he was surprised to see lamplight shining from a window in the house. Then across the stream he spotted a horse tied to the corral gate. The bunkhouse was dark, as it should be, for this morning he had sent Fred Harms to join Pete Weldin in pushing his stuff up into the Longbows.

With a kind of resignation Jim headed for the corral. Whoever was in the house could wait until he unsaddled and turned out his horse. By the time he had done this it was almost full dark, but as he passed the horse, saddle slung over his shoulder, he could make out the brand of the livery in town on the rump of its black hide.

He dumped his saddle over the sawhorse in the open-faced wagon shed, then passed the bunkhouse and crossed the twin planks that bridged the spring. Heading up the beaten path, he wondered what piece of law business was so urgent that it would bring whoever was waiting for him inside here at this hour.

He stepped through the door and halted abruptly. Kate Canaday, wearing a flour-sack apron tucked in at the waist of her skirt, stood with her back to the small stove, a ladle in her hand, watching him.

"Surprised?" she asked.

"That's a mild word for it," Jim said, taking off his hat and hanging it on the wall peg by the door. He asked, "Something come up, Kate? Any trouble?"

"None at all," Kate said. "Or maybe something did. Just plain female curiosity. We closed up early and I was free. I wanted some air, and I figured you'd probably come home after you left Triangle H. When I got here I realized you hadn't eaten since morning, so I fixed something."

Jim smiled. "Did you find the liquor?"

"Yes, but I was waiting for you."

Jim moved over to the open shelves and took down a bottle of whiskey. This was bachelor's spare kitchen, with a counter on either side of the sink where water was piped in from up canyon. A deal table stood against the wall and three barrel chairs were placed against it. On the other side of the wall was the bedroom.

"What did you find to cook?" Jim asked.

"Just what was in your cooler — steak, and

116

potatoes that were already boiled. You should have a garden, Jim."

"Yes, I suppose I could garden by lantern light. I've just never heard of anybody doing it. That's the only time I seem to have."

Kate laughed and Jim went over to the sink, mixed the whiskey with the ice-cold spring water and handed Kate her glass. They moved over to the table and sat down.

Kate said, "Everything is ready when you want to eat, Jim."

"Not right away." He smiled faintly. "I suppose you can't wait to hear what happened it the Big House. Well, it was a disaster."

He went on to tell her of finding Sarah alone and breaking the news of Cole's marriage. He described how her initial rage carried over when Cole and Bonnie showed up. He tried to describe it accurately up to where Sarah had ordered Ceferina to pack her things because she was leaving.

Kate listened without comment until he had finished. Then she asked, "How did Bonnie react to her welcome?"

"Like the cat that swallowed the cream. The cat knows they can't get the cream back, and Bonnie knows she's married. Also Bonnie knows that was the second piece of luck she walked into today."

"Sarah's leaving, you mean?"

Jim nodded. "Now she really is mistress of all she surveys, thanks to Sarah."

"You think it was only a tantrum, Jim? Don't you think she'll move back once she's cooled off?"

"I'd say not," Jim replied. "I think she'll stay mad and get madder, if that's possible." He smiled. "How did I describe her? 'A shy, sensible, high-minded girl.' "

Kate laughed. "I won't say it, Jim."

"You don't have to. I just wish you could read Bonnie the way you read Sarah."

Kate took a long sip of her drink while Jim rose and fixed himself another drink at the sink.

"Why does it matter to you, Jim?"

Coming back to the table, Jim said, "It couldn't matter less, Kate. It's just that I don't think I'm that bad a judge of character."

"And you think there's something wrong about Bonnie." It was a statement rather than a question.

Jim sat down, frowning. "Don't you ever get that feeling about people? It's not what they do or say, but it's something about them you sense. It's not rational at all, it's just there. I think it's more highly developed in women than in men."

"Yet I don't have it with Bonnie," Kate said.

Jim smiled and said, "I'm too hungry to talk any more about it, Kate."

Kate served their plain supper, and afterwards Jim helped her clean up and wash dishes. They were, Jim thought thankfully, fully talked out about the Hethridges, and they could talk of other things.

"If press day is your easy day, Kate, what's your rough one?"

"Monday, Tuesday and Wednesday, but especially Monday."

"Why that day?"

Kate, at the sink, looked sideways at him and grimaced. "That day Rich Sturdivant is getting over his weekend drunk. He does everything but tip over the type case, and I usually send him home in the afternoon and do his work myself."

"Yes, I've heard he makes the First Chance a weekend hangout," Jim said.

"That reminds me," Kate said. "Rich told me something that happened in the First Chance yesterday. Will-John Seton stopped in there in the afternoon and set up the house. Some Texan refused his drink and his cigar. Will-John put his gun on him, ordered a beer, poured it in the Texan's hat and then slapped it on his head."

"Sounds like him."

"Oh, that's not all. Will-John made the

119

mistake of thinking he had him bluffed. He put his gun away, paid for the drinks and started for the door. The Texan pulled his gun and stopped Will-John, ordered a pint of whiskey, and threw it in Will-John's face. Rich said everybody in the saloon whooped with joy at the sight of it. If I'd seen it I would have too. I don't like the man."

Jim was silent a long moment, and then asked, "You're sure this happened, Kate?"

Kate looked at him, rinsed the last dish, and took off her apron. As she wiped her hands she said, "No, but why would Rich make it up?"

"He wouldn't," Jim said thoughtfully. "Did he get the name of the Texan?"

"Keefe Hart. Why, is it important?"

Jim scowled and tossed the dishtowel on the counter. Then, head down, his hands in his hip pockets, he made a slow circle of the room. Kate watched him in puzzlement. When he sat down, she came over and sat down by him.

"You didn't answer my question, Jim."

He looked at her with a kind of somberness in his eyes. "Yes, it's important if you understand what's behind it."

"Why, it's just a couple of men making muscles, isn't it?"

Jim shook his head. "You see, the First

Chance is where the nesters and the poor cat-tlemen hang out when they're in town. It's the poor man's saloon. Every time Will-John Se-ton is in town he goes out of his way to stop by there. They hate him because he's Triangle H. He hates them because they run off his beef, cut his fences, steal his horses and want his range."

"Sort of an act of defiance?"

"Exactly. He'll buy them a round of drinks just to show his contempt for them. They ac-cept it and hate him for it. Now somebody has stood up to him and made him take water."

"Is Hart one of the nesters? I've never heard of him."

"Neither have I, but he did what every nester and two-bit cattleman has been want-ing to do."

"So Will-John might have learned a lesson. Maybe he'll stay away from the First Chance from now on."

Jim shook his head. "That's the last thing that'll happen. First Will-John will try to gun down Hart if he can find him. Whether he does or doesn't, he'll start pushing these poor outfits around. They've taken just about all they can from Will-John. If he crowds them they'll fight back, and we'll have a range war right in our laps."

Kate was silent a moment considering what

Jim had said. "I know most cattlemen envy Triangle H, but I didn't think there was that much feeling against it. Doesn't Seton know this will happen, Jim?"

"He won't care. He's got a hardcase crew and a big one. Besides, he's been challenged, and you don't challenge a king."

"You're close to both Sarah and Cole, Jim. It's their ranch. Can't you ask them to warn Seton before it's too late?"

"If they were a couple of other people I could. You see, Will-John has made them what they are. He's made them rich, and rich people are superior to the rest of us. They wouldn't warn him, Kate. They'd turn on me for suggesting it."

"Why haven't I heard these things?" Kate asked.

"You're not a cattleman. You've never been to the fall roundup. You haven't seen the look in a man's face when he sees hundreds and hundreds of fat Triangle H steers. Mixed in with them is his own cull stuff that's hardly worth shipping.

"Is there anything the *Banner* can do?"

Jim frowned. "Well, you could take sides when it busts loose."

"I already have," Kate said. She stood up and Jim got up too. "It's a work day tomorrow and I have to go."

"I'll ride in with you and stay in town."

"You'll do nothing of the kind," she said flatly. "I ride at night by myself three or four times a week. I just plain won't let you come with me, because it's foolish."

Jim smiled. "All right, but at least I can see you to your horse."

He took down the lantern from the nail by the door and lighted it, then led the way down the path and across the bridge and held the reins of her horse while she mounted. Handing them to her, he said, "Thanks for my supper, Kate."

"I should be thanking you, and I do, but I don't think I'll sleep very well tonight after what you've told me."

"Forget it. It's man's stuff. It won't touch you. Now good night, Kate."

9

In the chill early morning sunlight Will-John Seton, standing by the horse corral, gave the day's orders to a mounted puncher, who nodded and rode out. That left two men who had saddled up but not mounted. They were standing at the other side of the closed gate, and Will-John moved over to them and halted.

He addressed himself first to the taller of the two men, with a fight-scarred face and a badly set broken nose. "Les, I want you and Martin in town today. I want you to go to the First Chance. Find out from Tim O'Guy the name of the Texan that doused me with whiskey. He's tall, sandy-haired and mean-lookin'. Find him and bring him out here. You may have to travel, but don't give up on him."

"What if he don't want to come?" the younger puncher asked.

"That's why I'm sending two of you," Will-John said, as if that was sufficient answer to the question. Apparently the two hands thought so too, for they nodded and mounted.

Before they put their horses in motion, Will-John said, "He isn't a lad I'd like to tackle when I'm drunk. Don't you be."

They nodded again and rode out across country north.

Will-John, rope in hand, moved into the horse corral, which held a dozen horses from the strings of the various members of the crew. He walked across the corral towards his own bay and the other horses moved warily away from him.

His bay had long since given up the morning game of "You can't catch me," and stood motionless while Will-John slipped a rope over his neck and led him to the rope-chewed snubbing post. Will-John took a couple of turns of the rope around the post, then went to the gate that led to the horse pasture and opened it. He started a lazy circle of the corral, but the horses, knowing there was a day of loafing ahead, began to walk and then ran for the open gate.

Will-John went back to his horse, led it to the barn lot gate and then, his horse walking beside him started to the near wagon shed. His attention was attracted by a rider just circling the lake, and Will-John halted abruptly.

The rider was Sarah.

Will-John was thoroughly confused. Had

Sarah beat the crew awake to go on an early morning ride? He knew that wasn't possible. Her horse was a skittish devil, hard to rope even in the tight corral. He remembered that she'd asked one of the hands last evening to saddle up her mount for her customary sunset ride. Had she been out all night? That was to be expected of Cole, but not of his sister.

Sarah was heading for the rail in front of the office, and Will-John, not even bothering to fashion a hackamore, vaulted onto his bay and talked him into motion. He arrived at the tie rail just as Sarah reined in.

"Morning, Sarah." There was puzzlement in Will-John's voice as he went on, "You get up early, or you been out all night?"

"I spent the night in town," Sarah said crisply. She stepped out of the saddle and Will-John slid off his horse's back and took her reins.

"Will-John, can you spare me a man today?"

"The last two just lit out, Sarah. What can they do for you that I can't?"

"Why, nothing, I guess," Sarah said. "You see, I'm moving today. I'll need a team and the spring wagon."

"Moving where?"

"To Number Two."

Will-John scowled. "Why, the place has

been closed there, Sarah, since Mrs. Costigan died."

"Oh, I know it'll be dirty, but I'm taking Ceferina with me."

"You mean you're going to live there?" Will-John asked slowly.

Sarah took a deep breath and her brown eyes were quietly defiant. She said, "You might as well know it, Will-John. I won't live here any longer with that woman Cole brought home. I'll never sleep in this house as long as she's in it."

Will-John opened his mouth to say something and then thought better of it.

Sarah asked, "What were you going to say?"

"Only that the house is big enough so you wouldn't see her once a week unless you wanted to."

"No, it was my house and now it isn't. Will you move me?"

"Sure," Will-John said. He watched Sarah as she walked toward the house and he thought, *Well, I'll be damned.* He hadn't had a chance to see Bonnie last night or this morning, so he hadn't known what sort of reception Cole and his bride had received from Sarah. *I know now,* he thought. *There must have been a real row.*

He led Sarah's horse and his own back to

the wagon shed, tied Sarah's horse inside and saddled his own horse.

It took him half an hour to cut out a pair of horses in the horse pasture, put them in the corral, harness them and hitch them to the spring wagon. Afterwards he drove the team up to the house gate and, climbing down from the seat, noted that Sarah and Ceferina had stacked a huge pile of Sarah's gear on the porch.

As he made trip after trip to the wagon with valises and trunks of all sizes, he wondered how his own fortunes would be affected by this quarrel between Cole and Sarah. They both liked him and trusted his handling of Triangle H's affairs, but he understood enough of human nature to know there was a possibility that because one of them liked him the other one would start hating him, just to be contrary. He thought he could handle that, however. Cole, in spite of Burt Hethridge's and Will-John's own attempts to teach him some cow savvy, was next to helpless when it came to the business of the ranch.

Sarah was just as helpless in a different way. The crew didn't like her, but he had long since let the crew know that if they wanted to hold onto their jobs here, they would take Sarah's orders and not discuss her with him. What they thought of her among themselves he didn't want to know. Cole, of course, would start showing a little muscle to impress Bonnie but, with Bonnie's help, it would be easy enough to handle him.

Neither Cole nor Bonnie showed up when Sarah and Ceferina came through the door and Sarah closed it behind them. At the wagon Will-John helped fat Ceferina up onto the wagon seat and Sarah said, "Where's my horse, Will-John?"

"In the wagon shed. I'll get him for you after I've told Cole where I'm going."

"He knows," Sarah said contemptuously.

"All the same, I'll tell him again," Will-John said firmly.

From long custom held over from Burt Hethridge's day, Will-John went down the side of the house, climbed the steps of the kitchen porch and knocked on the kitchen door.

He was answered by Bonnie, who was wearing an apron over her calico dress. "Morning, Mrs. Hethridge," Will-John said politely.

"Come in. He's still asleep," Bonnie said.

Will-John stepped in, closed the door, took Bonnie in his arms and kissed her. She responded warmly, too warmly, and Will-John, knowing this was dangerous now, moved away from her.

"What happened?" he asked.

"Only a hell of a row," Bonnie said. "The duchess thinks I'm not good enough for her brother. She won't live in the same house with me."

"So she told me. I think you're lucky."

"Isn't Sarah waiting? We can talk later," Bonnie said.

"Yes. I want you to tell Cole I'm taking Sarah to Number Two."

"He knows."

"Bonnie, listen carefully. I want you to tell him that I told you I'm taking Sarah to Number Two, because I'm the only man around the place. You see what I'm getting at?"

Bonnie smiled faintly. "No favorites, is that it?"

"That's it. I'll try and make it back by dark."

The slow drive to Number Two was a dull chore that Will-John would not have wished on the greenest hand. Ceferina spoke only when spoken to, and what was there to talk to her about? Sarah, mounted and riding on Ceferina's side of the wagon, was as usual lost in some private world of her own. Will-John's horse was tied to the tailgate.

It was midday when Number Two ranch came into sight. The low alders of Officer Creek partially screened the one-story frame house. They approached the ford and jolted over its rocky bottom, and once the wagon was clear of the alders the house came fully into view. Nobody had ever bothered to paint it, and it had weathered to a uniform light brown color. Between it and the creek lay the log bunkhouse and cook shack, with the horse corral crowding the stream. In order to get Bill Costigan, the shrewdest judge of horse-flesh Burt Hethridge had ever known, Burt had had to build a house for his wife. After her death two years ago, Costigan had moved into the bunkhouse with the rest of the crew and left the house abandoned. It would, Will-John guessed, be a mess.

He drove the wagon up to the front door and got down, went up the porch steps and tried the door. It was locked. Somewhere down by the creek the sound of hammer on anvil came to him.

To Sarah he said, "I'll try the back door, and if it's locked I'll hunt up the key."

He tramped across the weed-grown yard, circled the house and tried the back door. He found it locked, and he headed for the bunk-house. It was empty, and smelled of unwashed clothes and sweat. He went past the bunks to the door that led into the cook shack, and in the narrow hot kitchen found the cook peeling potatoes. He was an old man, blind in one eye, and when he looked up and saw Will-John he gave him a toothless grin.

"Soda, how you been?" Will-John asked.

"Pore as hell," the cook answered.

"Well, you always were," Will-John said, and slapped him on the shoulder. "I'm looking for the key to the house, Soda."

"What for?"

"Sarah and her cook are going to live there. You know there the key is?"

Soda got up and brushed past Will-John, moved to the cook shack's outside doorway and lifted a key from a nail hammered into the log. Handing it to Will-John, he said, "Front door, Will-John. The back door's barred inside."

Will-John went back to the house, where the two women were waiting on the porch. He moved around them, unlocked the door and pushed it open. A blast of over-hot air struck him as he stepped inside. The sparse parlor furniture consisted of two rocking chairs, a sofa and a table. A coating of dust obliterated both the color and pattern of the rug and the upholstery. When he had gone across the room and yanked up the shade and opened the window, he turned and saw his footprints in the dust on the rug.

He looked up then at Sarah and caught the look of appalled distaste on her face.

Quickly he moved into the corner bedroom, opened both windows, and then went and did the same with the two windows in the small bedroom. Lastly he took the bar off the kitchen door and opened it, and opened both kitchen windows. The feathered skeletons of two birds trapped in the house lay on the floor and a hundred dead flies under one of the kitchen windows. There was a smell of birds and mice in the house that made him breathe through his mouth against the stench.

Turning, he went back into the parlor and saw Sarah leaning against the wall quietly crying, her face buried in her hands.

Will-John went up to her, tapped her on the shoulder and said, "It's not that bad, Sarah."

Then, to his amazement, Sarah threw her arms around his neck, put her face on his chest and began to sob. Will-John, scarcely knowing what to do with his hands, patted her on the back soothingly.

"Take it easy, Sarah," he said gently. "In a day you won't know the place." Looking over her shoulder, Will-John saw Ceferina unloading mop, bucket and broom from the wagon, and watched her disappear around the house, going toward the back door.

Sarah's sobs presently began to subside, and Will-John waited until she pushed away from him. Then he took off his clean necker-chief and held it out to her.

She wiped her eyes and cheeks and said in a quavery voice, "It's not the house, Will-John. It's just that I'm so lonely. Everybody has turned against me except you. Every *thing* has turned against me, too."

Inside Will-John something came alert. Sarah had never let him touch her when he was trying to court her, yet she had touched him today, and he had touched her, and it seemed that she now considered him her pro-tector and friend. Should he push it? *Don't,* something warned him. *Just coax it along.*

"It's been rough, all right Sarah, but if we can take the good, we can take the bad, can't we?"

His words, he knew, were simply a pious platitude and his "we" was meant in an edito-rial way. And now, almost in consternation, he saw Sarah come to his arms a second time, whether out of gratitude or helplessness he didn't know. Again he put his arms around her and stroked her back while she whim-pered quietly.

It was the sound of Ceferina starting to sweep out the kitchen that roused her. She looked up into Will-John's eyes and gave him a sad, friendly smile, then she sighed and said, "I'll have to get at it."

Will-John followed her into the kitchen. From under the kitchen table he pulled out a washtub and bucket, picked them up and stepped out of the back door with them. Dropping the washtub by the wooden-handled pump, he headed for the creek. There he filled the bucket and returned to the pump and carefully poured water in its primer. He gave the leather time enough to soak and swell and, when the water came, filled both the bucket and the tub. Afterwards he rummaged around the yard and found kindling enough to start a fire in the small kitchen stove. Sarah, he noted, had taken Ceferina off the job of cleaning the kitchen and they both were at work in what was to be Sarah's bedroom. Once the fire was going and the washtub was on the stove, Will-John went back to the wagon, tethered his horse to the porch post and began the chore of unloading.

The day was hot now and midway through the unloading Will-John's shirt was soaked, but he didn't mind it. He kept thinking how lucky he had been that he had sent off the crew before Sarah had asked for the loan of a hand. If someone else had made this trip in his place he would never have known the breakdown of Sarah's reserve. It wasn't a temporary breakdown, he knew now. Each time he came in with a load, Sarah, a towel pinned around her hair, would give him a friendly, almost conspiratorial smile, as if they shared a secret only the two of them knew.

Once the spring wagon was empty, he tied the reins of Sarah's horse to the tailgate of the wagon and drove it down to the big woodpile by the kitchen. Having unsaddled Sarah's horse and turned it into the corral, he returned to the woodpile, half filled the wagon with stove wood and drove back to stack the wood outside the kitchen door. After that he unhitched the wagon and turned the team into the corral. With the wagon unloaded and wood and water supplied, he knew the crew would give the two women any further help they needed this evening.

Back at the house, he went inside and halted at the bedroom door. Sarah, before the open trunk, was transferring her clothes to the curtained-off closet. Ceferina had started again on the kitchen. Sarah looked up as he stopped in the doorway, and again she gave him a smile.

"I'll be going, Sarah," he said. "When Bill gets in, tell him to have one of the men fill your lamps and send up some food. That ought to fix you for the night."

He moved into the room and stood with hands on hips, studying her. "You look happier."

Sarah nodded. "I am, but it looked so impossible at first, Will-John." Then she added quickly, "When will you be back?"

"Got to thinking a while ago," Will-John said soberly. "Now that you're out of the Big House, Sarah, why don't you come all the way out?"

Sarah looked puzzled. "What do you mean?"

"I mean now you'll be living like the rest of us in this country. Plain houses and plain folks around you. Why don't you do what plain folks do?"

"I still don't understand you."

"There's a dance at the Masonic Hall tomorrow night. I'll pick you up around four o'clock. Have Ceferina fix up a couple of box lunches. We'll dance all night, until you cry 'Uncle.' How does it sound?"

Sarah looked surprised. "I — I've never done it before, Will-John."

"You've never done this before either, have you?"

Sarah smiled. "I think I'd like it."

"I know you'll like it. Now get a good night's sleep tonight because you won't get any tomorrow night."

"I promise."

"Then see you tomorrow, Sarah."

She said good-bye and Will-John left. He mounted his horse, crossed the creek and headed up the road toward Triangle H. Today, he reflected, the course of his life had perhaps changed. Yesterday's humiliation had turned Sarah from a cold-hearted girl, headed certainly for old-maidhood, to a friendly, uncertain girl. The old arrogance had given way to a need for kindness and companionship. *And I'm just the man to supply it*, he thought calmly.

Already the old dreams of owning Triangle H were reawakening. If he played his cards right — and he would — Sarah would marry him, and he thought he knew how to handle his new Sarah. It would take gentleness and firmness, and it would have to happen while she was still vulnerable and feeling lost. A fast courtship and a sudden proposal wouldn't be such a bad idea. He had told her a hundred times that he loved her, so she would have no doubts on that score. And Cole's unexpected marriage to Bonnie had set a precedent. Being Mrs. Seton, wife of the man who really ran Triangle H, would give her an ascendency over Cole and Bonnie she had once had but had lost.

He knew with absolute certainty that if he married Sarah, he and Bonnie would own Triangle H. Their affair could continue if they were careful about it, but the beauty of it was that Bonnie was there to protect Cole's interest and Will-John would be there to protect Sarah's. In effect it would be his and Bonnie's money.

As he rode, he occasionally spotted small bands of cattle grazing in the distance, and he would cut over to look them over. When they moved away, calves at their side, he took notice of their glossy coats and wide haunches. His breeding was slowly paying off, he could see, and he felt a quiet pride in what would be his possessions.

He rounded the lake at Triangle H in the late afternoon. As he passed the bunkhouse he saw Les lounging in the doorway of the office. The sight of him augured bad news. Les and Martin had probably missed the Texan because of that single day of waiting. The Texan had probably inquired around and found out whom he had thrown the whiskey at, and decided it was time to drift.

Will-John rode up to the horse-pasture gate, turned his horse in and dropped off his saddle and bridle at the wagon shed. To his surprise, there were three horses tied in the shed out of the sun, and he felt a sudden thrust of excitement as he recognized Les' and Martin's mounts, but the big bay with a ladder brand on the hip was a stranger. Now he passed the bunkhouse and stepped through the open door to his office.

He halted abruptly. The Texan was seated on the worn leather-covered sofa against the far wall, his hat beside him. Martin was sitting in a straight chair watching him. Les was now seated in the swivel chair at the big roll-top desk, also watching. A shell belt and gun, obviously the Texan's, lay on the desk top. The Texan was glaring balefully at him, but Will-John studied him in silence for a moment, noting the patch of blood that discolored his sandy hair above his temple.

Will-John moved slowly into the room and halted. "You found out his name, Les?"

Les got up and stepped away from the chair and put his back against the wall. "Not from him. He don't believe in talkin'. Name's Keefe Hart."

"Any trouble?"

"Nothing we couldn't handle. Martin got the jump on him with his gun, but he wouldn't come along. I had to buffalo him. By the time we rounded up his horse somebody had called in old Andrews. He wanted to throw him in jail, but I said you wanted him out here. The sheriff didn't like it much, but we didn't pay him no mind."

"Cole here?" Will-John asked.

"Ain't seen him."

To Martin, Will-John said, "Go up to the Big House and see if he's there. If he is, ask

140

him to come over here."

Martin rose and left the room. When he was gone Will-John moved over to Hart and halted out of reach of him. "What are you doing here, Hart?" he asked mildly.

A corner of Hart's mouth lifted in a sneer. He did not speak. Will-John turned, and as he moved toward his desk he unbuckled his shell belt and laid it on the desk beside Hart's.

Afterwards he moved past the iron frame out against the wall into to a short corridor, whose closed door led into the bunkhouse. This corridor, perhaps three feet deep, served as his closet. On nails driven into the wall hung a worn slicker, sheep-skin coat, jumper, shirts and odd pairs of trousers. On one nail were a couple of belts, and Will-John took down one. It was a wide belt with heavy brass studs and a brass buckle. Trailing it from his hand, he walked back over to the desk and sat down in the swivel chair.

"Found out anything about him, Les?"

"He took a room over the First Chance. Paid up for month."

"Found out who he hangs out with?"

"Them nesters and cattle thieves that hang out there."

Will-John heard the sound of footsteps outside and turned to look toward the door. Cole, dressed in clean levis, checked shirt and half-boots, stepped into the room and halted. Martin stopped behind him. Cole looked at Hart, and then shifted his glance to Will-John.

"Who's that?"

Will-John said, "Name's Hart, a hardcase Texan. He threw a glass of whiskey in my face the other day in the First Chance. I had Les and Martin pick him up today."

"What for?"

Will-John rose. "Come outside and I'll show you."

He began to wind the brass-studded belt around his knuckles as he turned to Les. "Bring him out, Les."

Martin moved past Cole, and both he and Les converged on Hart. When they put their hands on him he rose and, with a man on either side of him holding an arm, he walked toward the door. Will-John placed his Stetson on the desk, and fell in behind them; Cole came last.

"Stand him up against the tie rail," Will-John called. By now the belt was firmly wrapped around his knuckles.

Les and Martin guided Hart to the far side of the tie rail and jammed him up against it, still holding his arms. Will-John circled the rail, with Cole trailing him.

Will-John halted before Hart and said, "Let him go."

Before either man could release their grip, Hart lashed out with a kick.

Will-John, anticipating this, took a quick step backwards and then said, "Throw him at me."

Les and Martin shoved at the same time, propelling Hart toward Will-John. Before Hart could even get his guard up, Will-John moved in with a savage hooking swing that caught Hart on the cheekbone with a violence that drove him to the ground. Hart rolled and quickly came to his feet facing Will-John, and was moving toward him. Hart's cheek, already cut by the brass-studded belt was beginning to bleed.

Then, as if he wanted to finish this one way or the other, and in a hurry, Hart lunged at Will-John.

Les, Martin and Cole moved in now, each guarding a flank, while the tie rail formed the barrier on the fourth side.

Hart's headlong charge Will-John dodged, tripping Hart as he moved past. Hart fell on his face, and Will-John made a cat-quick lunge at his prone body. Reaching him, Will-John dropped on him with bent knees and his weight drove an explosive bray of pain from Hart. Will-John rose now and kicked him in the side. Hart rolled away and fought to get to his feet. He was gagging for air, bent over almost double.

Then Will-John went to work on him in earnest. Time after time he drove his belted fist into Hart's face, and when Hart covered it with his hands, Will-John worked on his body until the hands came down and the face was unprotected again. Hart fought as best he could, but he was being driven back, and finally the tie rail caught him across the back.

Will-John was on him then with quick and savage cruelty. Unable to retreat, Hart could only try to cover his face and body. Blood was streaming from the cut on his forehead into his eyes, blinding him. He began to whimper now under Will-John's ceaseless blows. Will-John knew every trick of saloon fighting. He used his left arm for the blows directed at Hart's body and his belted right was aimed always for face and head. When Hart huddled into a defensive crouch Will-John would stamp on his feet then hammer with his belted fist on Hart's head and neck. Already Hart's shirt was wet with blood.

Will-John now straightened him up with an upper cut, and Hart put both hands back against the rail to keep from cartwheeling over. It was then that Will-John delivered the final blow. Hart's bloody face was totally exposed, when Will-John, with all his weight behind the blow, drove his belted fist into Hart's jaw.

The tie rail broke with the sound of a pistol shot under the power of Will-John's blow. The two halves parted and Hart instantly unconscious and unable to move his legs, fell heavily to the ground, the drive of the blow skidding him in the dust. He lay on his back, fists unclenched, palms up.

Deliberately, Will-John stepped over a broken half of the tie rail, halted beside Hart's right arm, then raised his booted foot and smashed the heel down on the palm of Hart's right hand. He did it twice; then, apparently certain that he had broken enough bones in Hart's gun hand to make it useless, he slowly began to unwind the bloody brass-studded belt.

Les, Martin and Cole came up now to regard Hart, in a silence broken only by Will-John's deep breathing.

When he had caught his breath sufficiently to speak, Will-John said, "Load him in the buckboard, Les. I want you and Martin to take him and his horse to town. Tie his horse in front of the First Chance, then throw him on the boardwalk. I want those nesters to have a look at him." Then he added as an afterthought, "Make sure they know I did it."

10

According to his custom, Jim made Saturday an office day. This was the day when the country people — the ranchers, dry farmers and the ranch crews — came in for supplies. Some drank and fought, but those who had litigation in mind or wanted legal advice came to see Jim.

Because they were country people as opposed to townspeople, Jim dressed as they did in clean range clothes, and because most of them wore guns, he wore one. However, the first thing he did when he unlocked the office was to take off his shell belt and hang it on a coat hook beside the door. He was in the act of doing that this morning when he heard someone coming up the outside stair. He went over to a window and opened it, and was moving toward a second window when he heard footsteps in the reception room, headed for his office.

He opened the second window and turned just in time to see Sheriff Andrews step through the door. "Morning, Harry," he said.

Sheriff Andrews was a tall, bent lanky man crowding sixty, whom Burt Hethridge decided long ago was harmless. His mustaches as well as his hair were full and white under a thin nose. Their lower edges were stained with tobacco juice, and as he came through the door his glance roved the room and settled on the cuspidor which Jim kept beside the armchair facing the desk. Sheriff Andrews walked over to it and spat generously into it. Now that he could speak, he said, "Got a minute, Jim?"

"Always. Sit down, Harry."

The sheriff was dressed in bleached levis and a buttonless vest to which was pinned the star of his office.

He sat down, took off his hat and laid it on the floor beside the cuspidor. Jim circled the desk and eased himself into the swivel chair. He guessed by the furrowed brow of the sheriff that something big was bothering him. To get something started he said, "Looks as if you've been missing sleep, Harry."

"Does it show that plain?" the sheriff asked; then he added, "Last night, for sure. You been in town much this week?"

Jim said wryly, "Too much. But what's been happening?"

"Well, it all started Wednesday afternoon. Will-John Seton paid his regular visit to

147

O'Guy's place. Some — "

Jim interrupted him. "I know all about it. Kate Canaday told me. Will-John had it coming. I'd sort of like to shake that Texan's hand."

"Not now, you wouldn't. Not after last night," Andrews said grimly. "Will-John waited a day, then sent in a couple of his boys yesterday. They got the jump on this drifter. Hart's his name. They took him out to Triangle H."

Jim scowled. "What for?"

"For Will-John to beat him within an inch of his life. The two hands brought him back in a buckboard. Dumped him on the walk in front of the First Chance. That was so them nesters could get a good look at him"

"Did they call you?"

Andrews nodded. "Me, before they called Doc Purcell. We took him over to Doc's place." He grimaced. "I never seen anyone beat up so bad, Jim. He looked like he'd been dragged face down behind a horse. His face looks like raw steak, his right hand is broke and so's his nose. Got an ear half tore off and some busted ribs." He finished by saying, "He damn near didn't make it through the night."

Jim said quietly, "What do you do now, Harry?"

"That's the teetotal hell of it," Andrews said. "What can I do? Burt Hethridge and Triangle H've kept me in office half a dozen terms. They never owned me, but I sure favored them over that trash that's tried to rustle them poor. If this Hart dies, I got to go after Will-John."

"What if he doesn't?"

"That's why I'm here, Jim. You know Will-John. You're the lawyer for the Hethridges. Can't you talk to him?"

Jim frowned. "And tell him what?"

"Why, that he's going to have half the country on his back, and pretty damn quick at that. You ought to hear the talk at O'Guy's place. They're murdering mad."

"But I don't see where I come into it, Harry. Tell Will-John what you told me. Better yet, tell the Hethridges."

"They wouldn't listen to me, but they'd listen to you."

Jim raised both hands palms out in protest and shook his head. "No, Harry. I'm done with the Hethridges. Once I turn over my accounts I'm through. That'll be today."

"But you're the executor of Burt's estate." He pronounced it "exec*u*tor." "That makes you boss, don't it?"

Jim shook his head. "Only of the money, and only temporarily."

"Can't you fire Will-John?"

"Oh, come on, Harry," Jim said in friendly derision. "If Triangle H's books showed he'd been stealing or mismanaging the spread, I'd have to report that to the court, and the court would advise the Hethridges. But Will-John hasn't done either of those things. He's a good foreman, and he's making them money."

The sheriff groaned. "Oh, God damn it!" he said softly.

"What are you afraid of?" Jim asked curiously.

"To begin with, I'm afraid of tonight."

"Why tonight?'

"That there dance at the Masonic Hall. Could be trouble there."

"Then tell Will-John that. You can't keep him away, but you can warn him."

"But you won't warn him?"

Jim only shook his head again. "Can't you get it through that skull of yours, Harry, that I don't want any more to do with Triangle H business? You're the law here. If you and your two deputies can't keep peace, turn in your badges."

"My two deputies," the sheriff echoed scornfully, "They see trouble coming, they just plain outrun it."

"Then get two who don't."

"I got a wife to live with," the sheriff said

sourly. "They're her nephews."

"Seems to me I heard a rumor they were."

The sheriff's face flushed. He reached down, picked up his hat, spat again in the cuspidor and then stood up. "Well, I figured you'd help me."

Jim said flatly then, "Harry, you've earned this trouble. You've stood by and let Triangle H haze these nesters off open range. You've let the big spread make its own laws."

"Hell, open range is for the man that can hold it," the sheriff said sharply.

"That's right. Let's see if Triangle H can keep on holding it."

"You used to work for Burt Hethridge. He sent you through law school. Now you turn on his kids."

Jim felt a slow wrath stirring within him. "I think I've paid back that debt, Harry. And I'm the judge of that."

"No, there'll be a lot of other judges," the sheriff said. He put on his Stetson, turned and slouched out of the office.

Jim rose and begin to pace the floor. Harry, he knew, had touched a sore spot when he had accused him of ingratitude. It was true he had spent much time, and therefore money, looking after Triangle H's affairs and settling Burt's estate. For this he had not even received thanks from Cole or Sarah or Will-John. But

151

now that Burt's two children were quarreling and Will-John was running rough-shod over weaker men, what business was it of his? The children were of age, and if they asked his advice, he would give it, but beyond that where was his obligation? For the dozenth time in the last two days, he decided he had none.

Halting at his desk, he reached in a lower drawer, drew out the letters and folders pertaining to Burt Hethridge's estate, and tucked them under his arm. He took his hat off the nail, locked his office and sought the street.

River Street was thronged, as it was every Saturday, with horses and teams and wagons. A wind was coming up, driving geysers of dust amidst the traffic. Jim remembered the open windows in his office and he looked down the street at the distant Longbows. The clouds told him some weather was piling in, but he judged it wouldn't come soon.

Turning in at the River House, he angled across its carpeted lobby, which held knots of men in conversation, and poked his head in the door of the small saloon. Judge Conover, as was his Saturday custom, was in a poker game with cronies he would not see for another week or month. He was a heavy, bald man, dressed in a rumpled dark suit. As if to compensate for his baldness, he sported a full pepper-and-salt beard, and jutting from its center was a cigar. The only time he was without one burning was when he was in his courtroom or when he was sleeping.

Jim moved through the crowded saloon towards the poker game and hauled up behind the Judge. He waited until the hand was finished and tapped the Judge on the shoulder. Judge Conover looked up and said, "Morning, Jim. Come to sit in the game?"

"Not with you, Judge. You're too tough. I've the Hethridge file with me. Want me to leave it for you at the desk?"

Judge Conover said, "Do that, but first I want a word with you." He rose and moved over to the corner and Jim followed him.

The Judge began, "Heard you paid off Cole's gambling debts. How did you cover them in your report?"

"Money due on notes held by Tom Dunning and Case Harvey."

"I don't have to acknowledge them as a legal debt against the estate, you know," the Judge said.

Jim nodded. "I know. You could strike them and let Cole pay up when the estate is settled — except for one thing."

"What's that?"

"When Cole gets his share of the estate, he wouldn't pay them. I think he owes them. As a hard-nosed poker player, do you agree?"

"I do." Judge Conover took the cigar out of his mouth and studied the ash for a moment, then he lifted his sad hound eyes to Jim. "However, I'm going to rule that half of that seventy-five thousand dollars is reimbursable to Sarah out of Cole's share of the estate."

Jim nodded. "I hoped you'd say that."

"All right, leave the file at the desk and let me get back to my game."

"Are they getting to you, Judge?"

The Judge snorted. "They're children," he said, heading back to his chair.

Jim left the file at the desk and sought the windy street, and already his mind was back on his conversation with the sheriff. For some unaccountable reason that conversation left him with a vague feeling of guilt. He wanted to talk it over with someone who would tell him honestly if he was wrong in feeling no obligation to Triangle H. Abruptly it came to him that he could discuss it with Kate, and on the heels of that thought came another. Why not ask her if she would go to the dance with him tonight, and afterwards they could talk.

He turned left heading through the hurrying, wind-pummeled crowd for the *Banner* building.

11

When Jim put the livery rig in among the saddle horses and teams stretched in a long line
before the tie rail of the Masonic Hall, the
evening sky was overcast and threatening. He
handed Kate down from the buggy and then
lifted her fancifully wrapped box lunch from
the seat beside his shell belt and gun. Kate accepted it, saying, "I wonder who I'll draw?"

"Well, it's always the drunk cow hands who
get the pretty girls, I've noticed."

Jim took her elbow and led her to a break
in the tie rail, and together they crossed the
boardwalk to the open doors of the big Masonic Hall. The skirts of her dress of ivory silk
billowed in the wind and she put her hand
down to hold the material against her legs as
she stepped through the doors. Abruptly they
were in the din of chatter from the hundred or
so people gathered inside. A dozen lamps in
wall brackets lighted up the hall.

A couple of women stopped Kate immediately, and Jim took her box lunch, made his

155

way through the crowd and deposited it on a mound of box lunches beside which the auctioneer was standing, looking at his watch. Already the room was hot, and Jim knew that before the evening was over it would be like a steam bath.

As he was leaving the table the auctioneer rang a hand bell, which was the signal for the women to move toward the chairs that lined the wall. There were twice as many men as women in the room, and now the men began to form a loose circle around the table. Most of the men were in clean range clothes, wearing the finest shirts they owned.

The bidding was about to begin and Jim looked over the crowd of men. Will-John Seton and Cole, along with a Triangle H hand, stood a little apart from the others. More men, after checking their guns in the coatroom at one side of the door, were crossing the floor to join the main group.

The auctioneer, who was chief of the volunteer fire department, told the crowd what it already knew: the money raised from the bidding for the box lunches was to go toward the purchase of a new hose-cart. After that the bidding began. In theory, no man was supposed to bid on the box lunch his partner had brought. When a man tried it the others would pounce on his bid with glee, raising the price until it was the equivalent of half a dozen hotel dinners.

As the bidding progressed, Jim looked over at the women seated against the wall. He was surprised to see Sarah Hethridge sitting next to Kate. Down the line, seated between two middle-aged women, was Bonnie Hethridge, who, as always, looked beautiful and smartly dressed. Jim wondered if she had chosen her dress of a fire-wagon red as befitting the occasion.

When one of the boxes took Jim's fancy, he bid on it against Sheriff Andrews and won. When the auctioneer called the name of the box winner, the shy young wife of the feed-stable owner stood up. Jim led her across the room to the row of chairs opposite the women's row where some of the couples were already eating from their boxes.

Always the easiest opening gambit was to ask a woman about her children, and Jim did this. The shy little woman gratefully rose to the bait, and while she talked about each child and how its traits differed from those of the others, Jim watched the room. He noted that Kate's box had been bought by a puncher who was in the act of unsteadily settling himself by her, and he smiled at the accuracy of his earlier prediction. He was wondering why Sheriff Andrews was dreading this night. There

were, to be sure, several of the small cattlemen present with their girls or wives, but they
all seemed friendly enough, and only out to
enjoy the evening.

When all the boxes were gone, it left about
fifteen womenless men and, predictably, they
drifted out through the door by the piano at
the back of the room which led to a corridor
that let onto the alley. Out there, Jim knew,
bottles and jugs would be passed around to
liven up the evening.

As Jim and Mrs. Carson finished eating,
the musicians came down the long room. The
four of them put their instruments on the table
and moved it into a corner, afterwards hunting out chairs, which they placed on either
side of the piano. The town's music teacher,
Mrs. Feldman, left her partner and took her
place at the piano.

Jim danced the first set with the little
mother of six and then took her to her husband. During the set, someone had brought
in mugs and half a dozen huge pots of coffee,
which were placed on the auction table. The
crowd was milling around the coffee now and
Jim joined it, trying to spot Kate.

It was then, over the clatter of cups, that
Jim and the others heard an exchange of shots
out in the alley.

The talk trailed off as more shots sounded,

158

and people looked at each other uneasily. On the heels of the last shot, a cow hand lurched through the back door and yelled, "They got Will-John cornered, by God!"

It was instinct rather than thought that turned Jim and headed him for the front door. By the time he had reached the door of the coat-room, he was running. He ran up the board-walk, found his rig, ducked under the the rail and reached on the buggy seat for his shell belt. Yanking his gun from the holster, he ran behind the line of wagons and saddle horses and started upstreet for the corner. As he turned down Bridge Street heading back to the alley, there was a savage exchange of shots.

He had almost reached the mouth of the alley when he saw a man crouched against the building, peering down the dark alley. As Jim hauled up beside him the man turned. Jim did not recognise him in the dark, but he could see the gun in his hand.

"Where is he?" Jim asked.

"He's forted up in that shed, across the alley from the hall."

Jim raised his gun, put the barrel against the man's temple and said, "Drop that gun and back off."

"Why you — "

"Drop it!"

He heard the gun hit the ground, and then the man rose and took two steps backwards. Facing him, Jim knelt, found the gun, turned and pitched it far down the alley. If the man wanted it he would have to pass Jim to get it. His back to the frame wall of the building, Jim moved slowly down the alley. He halted and called, "Will-John, it's me, Jim."

From behind the *Banner* building two doors past the Masonic Hall, a gun flash erupted and Jim heard the slug hit the building a couple of feet over his head. He shot at the gun flash, then heard a savage grunt, followed by a curse, and he crouched and moved forward. He was brought up abruptly by an unseen set of steps that raked his shins. He swung around the steps and squatted down in the dark corner where the steps joined the building. Now from the *Banner* door came two more shots, directed at the shed where Will-John was hidden.

"Will-John, answer me!" Jim called.

The answer was two shots that came from the flat roof of the Masonic Hall, and they were directed at him. They both hit the plank steps, and the second shot ricocheted off into the darkness with a whine.

Jim looked up and saw a figure on the roof silhouetted against the night. Whoever it was, was held by a second man, for he was leaning

160

out so far that if he had not been held he would have fallen. Jim carefully aimed and when his sight was lost against the dark figure of the man, he shot.

The man leaning out howled with the pain, his legs seemed to crumple and his body doubled over. For a second his companion held him, but then the man's weight was so far off balance that he had to let him go. The man turned a slow somersault in the air, and when his body hit the ground Jim could hear the great blast of air driven from his lungs. There came to Jim then the subdued murmur of excited talk from the back door of the hall. Then Sheriff Andrews called out, "Come out, Will-John. It's over."

"The hell it is!" Jim shouted. "Get that man off the roof, Harry."

Will-John's muffled voice came from across the alley. "Do it Harry, and hurry it up."

Jim rose, flattened himself against the wall, moved over to the hall's back door and called out, "I'm going down the alley, Will-John. Cover me."

"Right now," Will-John answered.

Jim knew the men in the hall's corridor had heard him. If anybody inside was of a mind to continue the fight, he'd given them an open chance at him by announcing his intentions.

Crouching low, he ran past the hall's back

door and kept on running, his goal the man in the *Banner's* back doorway. He was certain the second man on the roof couldn't see well enough to hit him on the run. He was expecting fire from the *Banner* doorway, but it didn't materialize.

Hauling up in the doorway, he stopped, looking up and down the alley. He could see nothing, not even the form of the man who had fallen from the roof. Out of curiosity he reached for a match in his shirt pocket. He found one and struck it alight on the *Banner* back wall. Looking at the alley dirt now, he saw the pool of blood and what seemed to be a knee print in it smeared by a fresh boot-print. Before the match died he thought he had the answer. One of the two men forted up here had been hit and downed. His companion had let off a couple of shots at the shed, then picked up the hurt man and hauled him down the alley out of gun range.

Sheriff Andrews' voice now called down from the hall roof. "There's nobody up here, Jim. Tell the boys to get a lantern lit down there."

Slowly Jim retraced his steps to the hall doorway, and before he reached it he saw the dim flare of matchlight, followed soon by the steady glow from a lantern that laid an oblong of visibility across the alley. In its light he saw a man's crumpled figure lying in the center of the alley. Against the shed beside the door a second body was sprawled.

Will-John called out from the shed, "Don't move out. Wait for Andrews."

It took only a minute before Sheriff Andrews, lantern in one hand, gun in the other, appeared in the doorway. He started across the alley and halted by the downed man in the alley's center. His glance lifted and he held the lantern higher to see the second man.

"All right, Will-John," he called.

The shed door opened and Will-John stepped out, blinking against the lantern light. As Jim moved toward him, he saw the wet left sleeve of Will-John's jacket with his bloody hand hanging from it.

Will-John looked first at the man against the shed, the Triangle H hand whom Jim had seen with him and Cole in the hall. Will-John knelt, turned him over and shook his head, then got up and moved to the center of the alley and looked down at the other man.

"I reckon that was an even trade," Will-John said tonelessly. Only then did he look at Jim and nod. "Thanks for the help, friend."

"Now, just what happened?" the sheriff asked. By now, men began to move out from the hall into the alley to see what had taken place. Will-John looked at them stonily, then

163

he answered Andrews.

"We come out to have a drink when they jumped us. Somebody struck a match and they opened up." He nodded towards the body against the shed. "Martin got it first, and then I got hit. I made the shed and stood 'em off until Jim came."

"How many?"

"Five, I'd reckon. Three down here, two on top of the roof."

"Likely Arly Green was the other one on the roof. Him and Shorty was always together." He looked at Will-John's dripping hand. "We better get you to the Doc now, Will-John."

Seton looked beyond him to Jim. "Come over to the Big House tomorrow morning, Jim. We're going to make medicine."

"I don't reckon I will," Jim said pleasantly. "It's a long ride from D Cross, and nothing will come of it, Will-John."

A fleeting surprise touched Will-John's face and he smiled faintly. "If you don't like that long ride, Jim, stay in town tonight. Tomorrow morning you'll pass by us on your way to D Cross. Stop in and say hello, will you?"

"All right," Jim said reluctantly. "It won't do any good, though."

Will-John nodded, and then called out, "Cole, walk me over to Doc's, will you?"

Cole stepped out of the crowd of men and

fell in beside Will-John who was already walking down the alley out of the lantern light. Jim was ramming his gun in his belt when Sheriff Andrews turned to him.

"What's your story, Jim?"

Jim told him briefly about disarming one man in the alley, exchanging shots with two men up the alley, and shooting Shorty Linder. He finished by asking dryly, "Now, what's your story, Sheriff?"

"What do you mean, 'What's my story?' " Andrews asked angrily.

"I know about your deputies, because you said if they see trouble coming they just plain outrun it. Looks as if you did too."

"My gun was in the coatroom!"

"You were expecting trouble tonight, so you left your gun in the coatroom. Will-John didn't leave his there or he'd be dead."

"I come as fast as I could."

"But not fast enough," Jim said. He turned now, heading for the back door of the hall, and the men watching parted to make way for him. In the corridor two men were barring the way of Sarah, and Jim heard one of them say, "You won't want to see it, miss."

Sarah saw Jim and said swiftly, "Is Will-John hurt, Jim?"

"Only a little," Jim said, and he brushed past her and stepped into the hall. The women were gathered in groups of three and four watching the corridor door. The musicians were silent, waiting for someone to tell them what to do. Jim picked out Kate at the far end of the room and as he walked toward her several women tried to stop him to ask what happened. Jim only shook his head and continued on until he came to Kate.

"I think we'd better go, Kate." Kate looked at him searchingly, then nodded, turned and moved toward the front door. They did not speak until Jim had handed her into the buggy, climbed in beside her, backed the buggy out and headed for the corner.

"Did they get Will-John?" Kate asked quietly.

"Hurt him, but not bad. They killed one of his men, and I killed one of them."

"Oh, no, Jim!"

"Oh, yes, Kate." Jim's voice held anger. When he realized it he added curtly, "Sorry."

"All right," Kate said humbly.

"Not now, Kate. I'll tell you later."

They were silent as they drove to Kate's home, a small frame house in the middle of a tree-shaded block. Kate foresightedly had lighted a lamp before she left, even though it had been daylight. Jim pulled the buggy up to the stepping block in front of the house, stepped down, walked around the buggy and handed Kate down.

"Come in with me, Jim. I'll make us some coffee."

"I'd like that," Jim said. He felt his anger and disgust with himself ebbing, although it was still there and would be for a long time, he knew.

Kate led the way up the back walk and into the house. They went into the tiny parlor, where the sofa and two chairs were strewn with books. She moved to the window and picked up the lamp, returned to the hall and led the way down the corridor, formed by closets on each side, and into a big kitchen. There was an oilcloth-covered round table against the window, and Kate, pointing to one of the chairs, said, "Sit there, Jim, where you can grind the coffee. I'll stir up the fire."

She moved over to a counter and took from the cupboard above it a coffee grinder and a sack of coffee beans, which she placed on the table. On her second trip to the cupboard she lifted down a labeled bottle of whiskey and a glass and set them by the coffee grinder.

She looked at Jim, who was still standing, and said, "Tonight, this is medicine. Take some."

"Join me?"

"No, but you go ahead."

Jim sat down, uncorked the bottle and

poured himself a generous shot of whiskey. Afterwards, while Kate was building a fire in the small stove and filling the coffeepot from the sink pump, Jim filled the coffee grinder with the roasted beans.

With the grinder between his knees, he went to his noisy work. He remembered then that his drink was untouched and he stopped cranking the grinder long enough to take a generous sip. Returning to his chore, he reviewed the events of the past hour, knowing that he had made a mistake and wondering why he had been driven to. There was no single reason why he should have involved himself tonight in this quarrel. It was not his fight, so why had he made it his?

Finished with the coffee grinding, he took the grinder over to Kate at the stove and watched her pull out the grinder's drawer and dump its contents into the enamel pot. Then, restless, he made a half-circle of the kitchen, saw his drink, halted and finished it. He looked over at Kate.

She was opening the back door, and when she saw Jim watching her, she said, "When I get rich, I'm going to build on a summer kitchen here. When it's warm outside, this can be an oven."

She came over now and sat down and Jim took his seat. He looked across the table at her. Her face was untroubled and he could see no resentment in it for him for yanking her away from the dance, or for creating the situation that had made it necessary.

"Kate, I did a damn fool thing tonight, and you know it. I'm trying to figure out why I did it."

"You mean going out for your gun?"

"So you guessed?"

Kate nodded. "When you headed for the front door, I knew you weren't going to break up the fight, you were going to join it."

"Yes. There was a man cornered out there that Burt Hethridge trusted. I worked with him. While I didn't especially like him, I respected him. He's too good a man to die that way."

"Well, it's done," Kate said with a simple matter-of-factness, "and you can't take it back." She added then, "You're not apologizing for your loyalty, are you?"

"It's a stupid loyalty, Kate. Or maybe I should call it an unthinking one. What was it that puncher yelled when he came through the door?"

" 'They got Will-John cornered, by God.' "

"That's what did it," Jim said. "He said 'they' and that meant more than one." There was disgust in his voice as he went on, "So I charge into something that Will-John set up for himself. I backed up his hand that I didn't like any part of."

"What'll happen now, Jim? What you were talking about the other night?"

"Pretty much," Jim said grimly. "Will-John will make a move and that will force them to make a move."

"And you're committed against your will. Is that it?"

"No, Kate. I'm not. I'm going to make it plain to both sides that I wouldn't stand by and see murder done. That's the only reason I moved tonight." He paused. "At least, I think, that's the only reason."

"You're not sure, then?" Kate asked quietly.

"Sure enough that I'm going to tell Will-John that tomorrow. He asked me to come to the Big House tomorrow morning."

"Of course he wants your help. He thinks he already has it."

"He won't after tomorrow. I'm going to tell him I'm the neutralest man he ever saw, and I figure to stay that way."

Kate smiled faintly. "Well, he can't make you join him, Jim. But if I read him aright, he'll figure if you're not for him you're against him."

"I won't let him figure that. You see, Kate, I'm one of the few men around here that isn't scared of Will-John and he knows it." He looked over at the stove. "There's our coffee boiling."

As Kate rose and hurried toward the stove Jim thought, *That's settled.* He didn't feel any better about the foolish thing he'd done, but now he knew what he was going to do about it.

Over the coffee, they talked over the pleasant part of the evening. Only once did Jim swing back to the unpleasant part, and that was to tell Kate that Sarah had been in the corridor after the shooting and that apparently the men there, probably out of a sense of fitness, had barred her from looking at the grisly scene in the alley.

"It's strange she'd want to see it," Kate observed, and Jim agreed.

His coffee finished, Jim rose and Kate came to her feet. "You riding out to your place tonight?"

Jim shook his head. "No, I'll stay at the hotel, since I promised to be at the Big House in the morning." He regarded her a quiet moment and then said wryly, "It was a gay evening for you, wasn't it? Full of fun and dancing with friendly people."

"You didn't make it what it was, Jim. Besides, there'll be other times."

"Lots of them, I hope."

Kate picked up the lamp, led the way through the house and paused in the hall, her hand on the doorknob. "You haven't asked me how I'll write this up for the *Banner*."

"No."

"Well, how will I?"

"Just the way it happened."

"I'll have to write that there are two factions, Jim. I can't print it without seeming to put you on the Triangle H side. And that will only make it worse, won't it?"

"This is Saturday, Kate. By the time you print the next *Banner*, I'll have made it pretty plain where I stand."

"Then let me know what happens. I want to be fair to you."

Jim nodded and Kate opened the door. She offered her hand and Jim took it, thanked her and said good night. Then he stepped off the porch into the windy night and headed for his rented buggy.

12

It was a windy overcast day when Jim rode into Triangle H just before mid-morning, but the almost certain rain was still holding off. A couple of Triangle H hands were lounging in the bunkhouse doorway watching a third hand shaving in front of the wash bench outside the door. They waved lazily to Jim, who said good morning and reined in at the office tie rail and dismounted. He was going toward the office door, when one of the punchers called out, "They're all up at the house, Jim."

Jim waved his thanks and angled toward the house, wondering what the man meant by "all." There were no horses at the house tie rail to indicate visitors. As he walked across the hard-packed ground, he glanced at the wave-chopped lake and saw that the wind had pushed the ducks into a small group at the east end of the lake.

The door of the Big House was opened by Bonnie before Jim could ring. She smiled, said, "Good morning, Jim," and held the door wide for him.

Taking off his hat, Jim moved into the parlor, then halted in surprise. Sarah, still in the dress she was wearing last night, was seated on the sofa beside Will-John. The foreman's left arm was in a sling, and as Jim entered he stood up. Cole sat in one of the easy chairs and he waved carelessly to Jim, who said, "Good morning, all." Bonnie, crossing the room behind him, said, "Sit here, Jim," and put her hand on an armchair facing the sofa, and then moved across the room to the desk chair.

Still standing, Jim asked, "How's the arm, Will-John?"

"Just a nick," Seton said, and he touched the sling with his right hand. "If I keep it in this, I don't even know it's there."

Jim sat down, put his hat on the floor and looked at each of them in turn. His glance finally came to rest on Cole, who, even though it was Sunday, was dressed in worn range clothes, as was Will-John.

"Family council?" Jim asked Cole.

"You think my precious sister would put her foot inside this house if it wasn't? Remember she wasn't going to set foot in this house again? Well, she slept here last night."

"Only because I had to," Sarah said somberly.

"You wouldn't let me wake one of the hands — "

"Cole!" Bonnie interrupted, and Cole didn't finish what he had started to say.

Will-John, still standing, took over. "Glad you came, Jim. We need you."

"Are you going to sue somebody?" Jim asked dryly.

"Not that way," Will-John said patiently. "We just need your help."

"Doing what?"

"Well, it looks as if this is out in the open at last," Will-John began. "Last night cinched it. They want a fight, and they'll get it"

"How?"

Will-John moved over to the desk and said, "Excuse me Mrs. Hethridge," and reached for a paper behind Bonnie. He glanced at it and said, "We've got twenty-eight hands working for us. That gives you and me fourteen riders apiece, Jim."

Bonnie said then, "I don't think we counted Jim's two hands."

Jim sat up straighter. "Did you say you and me, Will-John?"

Bonnie crossed her beautiful legs not visible under her skirt and said, "We settled on you instead of Cole, Jim. Cole wants to ride under you. He doesn't think some of the older hands would like to take orders from him.

Some of them helped raise him. So we all agreed on you."

"Again I ask, what is it you want me to do?"

"Why, between us we're going to push these nesters out of the country — our country."

"How?"

"With thirty-two hands, counting you and me and your hands," Will-John answered promptly.

"I don't mean it that way, Will-John. How do you propose to move a man off a place he's lived on for ten years? Shoot him?"

"They shot me," Will-John countered calmly.

"And you want me to take half your men and start a range war?"

"Call it that if you want."

"I have called it that, and I don't want it," Jim said. "Count me out of all of it."

The two Hethridges looked at Will-John, but Bonnie never took her glance from Jim. She broke the silence, speaking in a cold, almost implacable tone of voice. "You can't count yourself out, Jim, because you counted yourself in last night."

"Did I, now? I thought I went to the help of an old friend who was being ganged up on. That's all I thought."

"But you were backing up Triangle H," Bonnie said flatly.

176

"I was backing up Will-John Seton," Jim countered. "He's out of that particular trouble now. So am I."

Sarah said then, "But you've always helped us, Jim."

"I never helped you start a range war, and I don't aim to begin." He looked at Will-John. "I mean it Will-John. Count me out."

"When this gets warmed up, Jim, everybody will have to take sides. Does that mean you'll take the other side?"

"No, I won't take anybody's side."

Cole said then, "You've got a short memory, haven't you, Jim? You've forgotten everything Dad did for you."

Jim felt a swift anger and tried to hide it. He said slowly, "Not for a minute, Cole. As soon as I could, I paid back the money it took to send me to law school. The same goes for the beef to stock my range. I've handled your business the best I knew how. No, I haven't forgotten."

Bonnie put in quietly, "Then give us the real reason you won't join us, Jim. Is it because you think we're wrong?"

"Yes."

"You better explain that, Jim," Will-John said.

"All right. I think Burt Hethridge was a hard man, Will-John. Not to his friends,

177

Lord knows, but to the rest of the world. Whenever he could, he took from the weak. He took more than he needed, more than his share. He held it with guns, just the way you're trying to hold it, but you can lose it at gun point too."

"Are you sayin' we should give in to these nesters?" Will-John asked contemptuously. "After last night are you sayin' that?"

"Not give in, just pull back some of that open range. All they want is room enough around to raise enough stock."

"What's enough?" Bonnie asked coldly.

"Enough so they won't have to rustle your beef, because they'll have grass of their own."

"So I forget they shot at me?" Will-John asked angrily.

"You've got yourself a tame sheriff, Will-John. Let him find out who went for you last night. That shouldn't be hard. Let him arrest them and try them for murder, because they started the fight."

Will-John shook his head in angry disbelief, and when he spoke it was with withering sarcasm. "First you want us to give up our land. That's the reward for killin' one of our men. Then you want us to go to court. Why, we'd be laughed out of the country."

"No, you'd be respected. Whoever killed your man can be caught and convicted. They

178

call that 'due process of law,' Will-John, in case you've never heard of the phrase."

"Go down to the bunkhouse and tell my men that. See what they say."

"Why don't you go down and tell them?"

Will-John snorted. "They'd quit before noon, to a man. If I can't protect them and even the score, why would they work for me?"

"The score is even."

Will-John smiled without humor. "No. A jack-leg lawyer evened the score, a man who ain't even on our side."

Jim reached for his hat and stood up.

"Last chance, Jim."

Jim shook his head. "No, I'll sit this one out, Will-John. Good day to you." He moved to the door, opened it, and leaving the porch, headed for his horse. When he was mounted, he put his horse around the lake, crossed the stream and started toward D Cross.

He hadn't made much of a case for himself, he supposed, but at least they knew where he stood. Cole and Sarah, of course, would stand behind Will-John. The arrogance of power, if nothing else, would push them into backing him. They had grown up expecting, demanding and receiving anything they wanted. It would be as unthinkable to them to give up even an acre of ground to a pack of rustling nesters as it would be to let the death of a Triangle H hand go unavenged. This is what Burt Hethridge had taught them and Will-John had enforced.

And somehow during Bonnie's short acquaintance with Triangle H, she had absorbed the same philosophy. That was understandable in a woman who had had little and suddenly had acquired much and wasn't about to part with it. From her manner of questioning him instead of letting Cole take over this chore, Jim thought he knew who was the boss in that marriage.

He could not shake off a feeling of gloomy fatalism. If Will-John carried out what he planned with his twenty-eight hands, this country would erupt into a savage war. Men would strike and take to the back trails, and other men would retaliate. Predictably, there would come a time when only the women and children were safe, and men who had never worn a gun would be packing one.

One side knew his position. It wouldn't be difficult to tell the other side. A single visit to the First Chance and a few words with Tim O'Guy would suffice. Shorty Linder had brought on his own death, since he had chosen to shoot fist. Jim knew that it was a very narrow line he must walk. He also knew that it would be easier to convince the townspeople of his neutrality than the ranchers of the country. They would all take sides sooner or later and would try to pull him to join their side.

It was sometime in early afternoon when he first smelled, but did not see, smoke. His first thought was of a grass or forest fire, and as he looked west at the distant Longbows he saw the clouds were unloading in the high country. The west wind would drive them this way to put out any fire.

But as he rode on into the afternoon, the smell of smoke became stronger. He was certain now that it was not a grass fire but was wood burning, and he felt a certain relief. A grass fire could clean out his winter range, he knew. He had seen grass fires pushed by a wind like this that would outrun a horse and, like all other cattlemen, he dreaded it.

He picked up the D Cross road and the smell of smoke was even stronger. A faint apprehension prodded him into lifting his horse into a trot, and then his own valley lay directly ahead of him. The smell of smoke was still stronger now. There had been no rain here and probably no lightning to touch off a fire, and this thought increased his uneasiness.

When he reached the familiar spot in the road where he could see the roof of his house, he saw the roof was missing, and he felt a dread grip him. Lifting his horse to a full gallop, he topped the small rise from which all of his buildings were normally visible. There was nothing standing. The house had burned to the ground, as had the bunkhouse and wagon shed. The rock and mud chimney of the fireplace in his living room was still pointed to the sky. The iron kitchen stove had been tipped on its side by falling roof timbers.

As he came closer, he saw the full devastation, and the sight sickened him. Reining in by the bridge, he dismounted and surveyed the scene. Beside the overturned kitchen stove a length of pipe with faucet attached stood where the sink had been.

Crossing the bridge, he halted in the middle of it, his attention caught by an object in the shallow water. It was the five-gallon can that held his coal oil, and he thought with rising fury that this undoubtedly had been used to start the fire. The logs of the walls had collapsed outwards and were almost entirely consumed. The base logs were still smoldering. Almost every log had been burned; only odd bits of metal had survived what must have been a holocaust. Everything he owned except his stock, the clothes on his back and the books and furnishings of his town office was gone.

He came closer and he could feel the still warm earth through his boots.

Turning then, he crossed back over the bridge to the bunkhouse. It was leveled too. In the wagon shed only odd bits of strap iron that held the wagon and buckboard together remained. One side of the corral beyond was burned out; the rest of the corral stood, although some of the logs on either side of the gap were all smoldering.

Standing there, his fury close to choking him, he tried to piece together what must have happened. With both Pete and Fred raising the line camp shack on his lease in the Longbows, D Cross had been deserted. Whatever man or men had set the fire must have known he was in town. Undoubtedly his defense of Will-John Seton and his shooting of Shorty Linder had triggered the act. They must have made their decision immediately after the fight and ridden out to D Cross. Without a doubt they had soaked the interior of the buildings with the coal oil and touched off the fire, and the persistent night wind had done the rest. His closest neighbor, Parker, four miles away, had a place on the creek bottom, and even if he had been awake outside, he still wouldn't have seen the flames.

Three hours ago, Jim had righteously proclaimed his neutrality, certain that he could maintain it, yet even while he was talking he was becoming the victim of a range war he wouldn't be drawn into.

As he stood there, his bleak anger riding him, the first drops of rain fell. Moving over to his horse he took down his worn slicker from the saddle, unrolled it and shrugged into it, and then in the beginning drizzle he began cruising around the ruins looking for some clue as to who had done this. As the first rain drops struck the base logs they made a hissing sound over the rush of the wind.

Starting with the bunkhouse, he found a blurred set of footprints leading to what had been the doorway. They were made by big boots, but Pete was big and they could have been his tracks.

Now it began to rain in earnest, and Jim moved over to the corral. There was a strange set of horse tracks on the far side of the corral, but they were made in trampled grass that blurred any distinctive markings the shoes might have had. The rain, he knew, would wipe them out in minutes. Circling the ashes of the bunkhouse, he came back to his horse and mounted. There was nothing here that could point to the identity of the arsonist. He put his horse into motion and headed back down the road, his shoulders hunched against the wind-driven rain.

Now he tried to sort out the alternatives before him. He could ride back to Triangle H and tell Will-John he had changed his mind and would throw in with them. Yet the ensuing fight, with or without him, was just as senseless as he had described it this morning. Why should all of these sorry nesters be hunted down for the actions of one or two of their number? Or he could ride into town and learn what progress Harry Andrews had made in learning the identity of the men involved in last night's fight, and take it from there. . . . Or he could forget the whole thing, and with Fred and Pete rebuild the D Cross, letting it be known he was neither friend nor enemy to either side.

The first and last choices were really no choice at all. He would not be identified with Triangle H, and on the other hand he would not turn the other cheek. He would hunt down the man or men who had fired D Cross. He would, of course, be accounted a friend of Triangle H, but it was up to the sheriff and himself to set that straight.

As he rode through the driving rain, he felt bitterness, which he correctly diagnosed as self-pity. True, he had lost a home he liked and was used to and was proud of, but that was replaceable. His real but modest wealth was in his cattle and in his lawyer's mind. They were enough.

185

13

It was already raining when Will-John, with Sarah in a borrowed slicker, set out for Number Two in the top buggy. Sarah hadn't wanted him to drive her, saying that he should rest and that any of the Sunday-idle hands would be glad to do it. Will-John had scoffed and then said he had to go to Number Two anyway to sort out the crew he wanted, and besides he must ready Number Two for the inevitable attack by the nesters.

When they left Triangle H, the splash curtain had been rigged up for them, and with it pulled over their legs there was a strange sense of intimacy between them. Will-John felt it, and he knew from the way Sarah sat so close to him, her thigh against his, that she felt it too. He recalled how Sarah had reacted to the attempt on his life last night. He and Cole had no sooner reached Doc Purcell's office and he had stripped off his jacket and shirt, than Sarah came knocking at the office door. Doctor Purcell barred her way and ordered her to stay in the parlor until he was finished. Once Will-John's flesh wound was cleaned and dressed and his clothes back on, he went out into the parlor, Cole following. Sarah, he saw, had been crying and when he entered she had rushed up and hugged him, indifferent to the audience.

On the way back to their buggy, tied in front of the Masonic Hall, she had held his arm. When he had told both Cole and Sarah with brutal directness that they had better forget their quarrel and unite for common protection, Sarah had squeezed his arm and said, "Of course, Will-John." He had added that the drive to Number Two that night was idiocy and that, like it or not, she was to accept the hospitality of the Big House one more time. Again she had agreed, and on the drive out there she still held his arm. She even saw him to his bed in his office. It was as if, last night, she had discovered with a frightened panic that only Will-John stood between her and the very cruel world. At breakfast, she had hovered over him solicitously, cutting his meat, pouring his coffee, totally oblivious of Cole's sneering attitude.

There would never be a better time than now to make his proposal, he knew. She was worried about him and completely dependent upon him.

"You're awfully quiet, Will-John," Sarah said. "Is it beginning to hurt?"

"Not my arm. Maybe my conscience."

"What about?"

Will-John turned his head to look at her. "Why, you, I reckon, Sarah. You haven't got any idea of what's ahead of you, have you?"

"You mean, outside of loneliness? No, I guess I haven't."

"I know too damn well, and I don't like it. I'll leave at least four men with you at Number Two, because I'll be gone most of the time. But even they can't guarantee you'll be safe. Sooner or later, they'll hit the place and burn it down on you, if they can. You don't belong way out there, by yourself." He added grimly, "If anything happened to you, I'd shoot myself."

"But where is there to go, Will-John?" Sarah asked in a small voice.

He had succeeded in adding to her fright, he saw. A sudden gust of wind drove the rain against the buggy top with a drumming sound, and Will-John waited until it eased off before he answered.

"Listen to what I say real careful, Sarah. Don't answer right away." He paused. "You know I've been in love with you since you cut off your pigtails. I've asked you to marry me before, so you won't be surprised if I ask again. We should get married, Sarah. You need a man, and not just any man. You need me. Tomorrow we drive into town and have the Judge marry us, like he married Bonnie and Cole. Then we put you up at the River House. You'll stay there and look for a house you like in town. I'll see that you're moved and made comfortable there. I want you with people, a lot of people. You won't be that rich Hethridge girl any more, you'll be the wife of Will-John Seton. And he, by God, will kill any man that bad-mouths you or touches you."

"Yes," Sarah said immediately.

Will-John looked at her in genuine surprise. "You mean it?"

"I mean that one word."

"I told you to think it over before you answered."

"I thought it over long before you asked."

Will-John clamped the reins between his knees, put his arm around her, drew her to him and kissed her. Her lips seemed to dissolve wetly against his and he knew that if he was alone with her at home he could have her.

"Oh, Will-John," she finally whispered, "will tomorrow ever come?"

Next morning came clear and cool, smelling of mud and washed grass. After his breakfast in the River House dining room, Jim picked up his bay at the feed stable and rode over to the brick courthouse. As he dismounted in the side yard at the tie rail under the cottonwood, he heard a window being raised and looked across his saddle. Sheriff Harry Andrews was at the window; he could have seen Jim and called to him, but instead he turned away, probably remembering Saturday night. Jim rounded the rear corner of the building and heard the other window of the sheriff's office being raised. Harry was preparing for a hot day, Jim thought grimly, and he himself was just the man to start warming it up for him.

Entering the rear door of the corridor, Jim took the first door to his right and was in the sheriff's square office. Sheriff Andrews had seated himself, and at Jim's entrance he slowly swiveled his chair away from the battered rolltop desk to face his caller. Their last two conversations had been angry ones. His long face seemed to indicate he didn't want this one to be. He even smiled. "Well," he said, "you're in pretty early, Jim. You must have started out before daylight."

"I stayed in town last night, Harry. Know why?" He didn't wait for the sheriff to ask him to sit down, but went over and took the straight-back chair by the desk.

"No idea." The sheriff's tone was cautious.

"Because my place is burned to the ground."

The sheriff's shaggy brows lifted in surprise, and then he asked, "A set fire?"

Jim nodded. "For sure. The only thing that wasn't burned was the coal-oil can they used to start the fire."

"When did this happen?"

Jim told him it was Saturday night, reminding him of Will-John's request in the alley for him to come to Triangle H on Sunday and of his refusal, of Will-John's suggestion that he stay in town that night and drop in when he passed by the next day.

"I remember."

"Anyone in that crowd could have done it Harry — anyone that hates Triangle H."

"There was a lot of them there."

"Did you find out who I shot in the alley behind the *Banner* office?"

"I never heard, Jim."

"Did you try to find out?"

The flush of anger darkened the sheriff's face. "I tried, but Sunday's no day to find out anything. Folks mostly visitin' other folks. You could spend the day tryin' to find a man."

"You try O'Guy's place?"

"First off, and three times yesterday. They stayed away yesterday. They know that's where we'll look for 'em first."

"Did you check with Doc Purcell?"

"I done that too." Andrews put his hands on the desk and looked resentfully at Jim. "I can't figure you out, Jim. I come to you to ask you to warn Will-John away from that dance. You wouldn't do it. Then when they corner Will-John Saturday night, you're there fightin' for him. They burn you out for backin' him. Now you're here ridin' me for not bringin' in a man who was shootin' at you. What do you want from me, Jim?"

Jim looked at him searchingly and then said, "A deputy's badge."

Andrews looked honestly startled. "What for?"

"You won't like the reasons, Harry."

"I never like much of what you say, but say it."

"All right. First you should've been on top of that fight Saturday night. You weren't. You know five men were involved in Joe Martin's murder and Will-John's shooting. You and your two deputies aren't even looking for them. Where are your two deputies, by the way?"

"They'll be in later on."

"Why weren't the three of you riding your tails sore yesterday to find out who planned that ambush and who was in it?"

"I told you — "

"You told me," Jim said derisively. "Harry, this whole country is going to blow up in your face, and you'll let it."

"How can I stop it?"

"Find those four and arrest them for conspiracy to murder. If you can't or won't, I will and can. That is, if you deputize me."

Sheriff Andrews rose with an abruptness that sent his swivel chair rolling on its castors a good eight feet. His gaunt face flushed even more, a brick color against the white of his mustaches.

"I can't do it, Jim, and you damn well know it! That's giving you and the whole Triangle H crew a hunting license to kill anybody you don't like."

"Why tie me in with Triangle H?" Jim asked quietly.

"Tie you in!" the sheriff said explosively. "Why, you gunned down a man trying to get Will-John."

"If you'd been where you should've been, you'd have gunned him down, too." Jim said. "Look, Harry, yesterday Will-John asked me to throw in with them. I told him no. I'll tell him no again even after I'm burned out. I don't want anything to do with Triangle H. I told you that Saturday afternoon, in case you've forgotten."

"You fought for Will-John that night. How come?"

"I won't see any man I've worked with and respect ambushed in a dark alley. That doesn't mean I'm his man or anybody's man."

"Then why do you want to be deputized if it ain't to give Triangle H a bulge on them nesters?"

Jim said, "Ah!" with a fathomless disgust; then as if explaining to a child he said, "You and your two deputies can't find the man I shot. I can, but I can't arrest him. You and your two deputies can't find who burned me out. I can, but I can't arrest them. Can't you understand that?"

"I can, but it ain't true."

Jim rose now and said quietly, "Prove it isn't true. Let's go find the man I shot. Right now. Lock up the office and let's go."

"I got a dozen things I got to do here in town today."

"Sure you have," Jim said, "today and every day. So have your deputies, if they bother to come to work." He paused. "You coming?"

The sheriff went over to his chair, trundled it back to the desk and sat down. He was, Jim knew, not about to accept the challenge.

"I ain't got the money for another deputy. I'll have to see if the Commissioners will let me hire you."

"I don't want any money," Jim said. "You

don't have to see the Commissioners either. You can deputize any man on the spot, and you know it."

The sheriff said sullenly, "Damn you lawyers, anyway."

"And damn you sheriffs," Jim said mildly. "Want to swear me in now, Harry?"

The sheriff sighed. "All right. But I don't like it. You try and pull a fast one on me, Jim, and I take the badge back."

"Whatever I pull, you can be sure it'll be fast. Now hurry it up, Harry."

The sheriff reached in a right-hand drawer of the desk and took out a badge, searched for and found a crumpled piece of paper, which he unfolded. "Raise your right hand," he said.

Jim swore that he would support the Constitution of the United States and this state and would perform the duties to the best of his skill and ability, so help him, God.

Andrews handed him the badge, which Jim pocketed.

"Thanks, Harry. Now let's us play a game."

"What game?"

"Nobody knows I'm burnt out except you and whoever set the fire. You keep your mouth shut about it. So will I, except for telling one other person who won't talk. Let's see who's the first to tell us about it."

"Who's the other person?"

195

"My business," Jim said, and he turned and left the room.

Outside, he mounted his bay and headed for River Street. He had what he needed now, although it had taken some doing. He thought with a full measure of pleasure that Harry Andrews was serving his last term. He could never survive what was sure to come, let alone stay on top of it.

River Street still held pools of water from yesterday's rain and he had to skirt a big one in front of the *Banner* office, where he reined in and tied his horse.

When he went inside and through the counter gate, he saw Kate in conversation with Rich Sturdivant under the lamp by the type case. The clack of the closing gate made her look up and see him. She came through the low shop gate to her desk. There was no apron over her maroon-colored dress this morning and she was wearing a pillbox of a hat. Jim guessed she had either arrived late for work or had been out soliciting advertising.

Kate said. "Morning, Jim. I didn't think this was one of your days in town.'

As she took off her hat and put it on the desk, he said "Well, it's not every day I get made a deputy sheriff."

Kate looked searchingly at him. "You're not serious, are you?"

For answer, Jim reached in the pocket of his jacket took out the badge and laid it on her desk. She looked at it and then lifted her glance to him. "Why?"

He slacked into the chair beside the desk, took off his hat and laid it on the desk, covering the badge. "I've got a couple of chores for Harry to do that he won't do. With this badge, I can do them myself."

Kate frowned. "What chores, Jim?"

"Well, one is to find out who the four men are who tried to bushwhack Will-John and who killed Martin. The other is to find out who burned down my place Saturday night."

Kate's lips parted in the shock of her surprise. "Oh, Jim, that can't be true! It *can't* be!"

"All the buildings are level with the ground," Jim said tonelessly.

"But why, Jim, why?"

"I reckon it's because I backed Will-John's hand Saturday night. I can't think of any other reason." He told her then of the number of men who had heard him say he was going to stay the night in town. Any one of them, hating him for siding with Will-John, could have chosen this swift retaliation. As he talked, Kate nodded.

When he had finished she said bitterly, "Or anyone who heard it could have told a dozen people." She paused. "Isn't anything left, Jim?"

"Three-quarters of a corral and a five-gallon coal-oil can."

"How foul!" Kate said quietly. "It's like shooting a man in the back."

Jim smiled crookedly. "Want to hear the real twist of the knife? Yesterday, I told Will-John and the Hethridges I wouldn't throw in with them."

Kate hesitated, and then asked, "Will you now?"

"No. The fire doesn't change anything. It doesn't make right what Will-John plans to do, does it?"

"I don't know what that is."

"Divide twenty-eight men into two gangs and fight those nesters any way he can. That will surely include murder."

Kate nodded and then said, "Your news makes mine sound a little tame, Jim. Will-John and Sarah got a marriage license this morning. Just before you came in I checked with Judge Conover. He married them about an hour ago."

Jim sat in a stunned silence. It came to him then that Will-John, in effect, now owned all of vast Triangle H. Cole was a cipher, and so, in effect, would Sarah be. After yesterday's meeting at the Big House, it was plain that

Bonnie ruled Cole and was backing Will-John. For better or worse, Triangle H was now the property of Will-John Seton and that expert little dressmaker, Bonnie.

"Sarah had to turn to somebody, Kate. Why not Will-John? Cole's a nothing, and I backed off. I'm guessing she saw the trouble ahead and couldn't face it alone."

Kate said, "That trouble just might start today, Jim. I stopped by the hardware store and talked with Hank Woodward about the burials of Joe Martin and Shorty Linder. Their funerals are both this morning. Joe Martin's at ten-thirty; Shorty Linder's at eleven, in a pauper's grave."

Jim knew exactly what she meant without her having to explain it. Will-John, with the whole Triangie H crew, would show up late. Without them, there could be no burial service. The nesters would come only minutes after Triangle H. Shorty Linder was a single man, as was Joe Martin, and since neither had a family here, nor came from here, that meant there would be no women at the funeral. It was, Jim realized, a made-to-order chance for Will-John. Out of pride and defiance, the nesters would come to see Shorty buried. Triangle H and Will-John burying one of their own men, who had truly been foully bushwhacked would be mad, tense and eager.

"Don't you go to the cemetery, Kate."

"Don't you go either. Who killed Shorty Linder?"

Jim came to his feet. "Did Hank tell Harry Andrews about the times of the funerals?"

"That's something I didn't ask him. He only seemed anxious to get them underground."

"Then I'll back-track and tell Harry," Jim said grimly. He picked up his hat and badge and started for the door, but halted. "Kate, only the sheriff, the man who burned me out, and I know about my fire. You make four of us. If none of us talks about it, let's wait and see who tells us about it."

"All right" Kate said. "Where do I reach you now, Jim?"

"The River House." Jim found himself hurrying through the counter gate and out of the door to his horse.

Once mounted, he pulled his bay around and started back toward the courthouse. In view of last Saturday night's fight, Hank Woodward must have been out of his mind to schedule these two funerals so close together, he thought. He wondered grimly how Harry Andrews would handle this, or if he would even try to handle it.

At the courthouse he went to the sheriff's office and found the door locked. His knock brought no response, and he stood there in the corridor wondering how to interpret the sheriff's absence. Had he heard of the closeness of the two funerals and gone up to the cemetery? Or was he out on other business, unaware of the explosive situation building up?

As a deputy, Jim had worn a badge for only twenty minutes. It would be presumptuous of him to assume a duty he had not been assigned. On the other hand, he couldn't afford not to assume that duty, and he could not be sure that Harry Andrews was out at the cemetery.

He went outside, mounted his horse and started for the cemetery half a mile west of town.

14

It wasn't exactly an economy move that led Hank Woodward to place Shorty Linder's and Joe Martin's plain pine coffins in the black hearse together. It was the element of time that dictated this. It would be impossible to bury Joe Martin, starting at ten-thirty, drive the team back to town, pick up Shorty Linder's coffin and return to the cemetery by eleven o'clock. The friends of both men had specified there should be no church service, only a brief graveside ceremony.

Shortly after ten Hank drove through the cemetery gates and looking through the tall cottonwood trees that shaded the graves, he saw the sexton, Seth Miller, dressed in the same sort of decent black suit he himself was wearing, seated on a headstone beside the mound of raw earth. It was, Hank thought, too nice a day, even for one funeral, let alone two. And, unlike Seth Miller, Hank, as each year added to his middle age, had come to hate funerals, for they reminded him of his own mortality.

He was a slight man, possessed of a wry humor, and the only reason he was an undertaker was that it was expected of a hardware merchant as his duty to the community. In the fifteen years he had been here, he had buried perhaps half the dead in this cemetery. They had ranged from babies to Civil War veterans. He had ordered their tombstones and the ornamental fences that surrounded some of the graves, and in the proper season he had decorated the graves with his own flowers.

As he reined in the team on the road before the open grave, he saw that Seth had everything arranged. Two heavy boards stretched across the open grave.

"Catch yourself some blisters yesterday, Seth?"

Miller, a bearded and sour man, said, "Nope, but I like to sprung my back. I was shoveling nothing but mud for half the day."

Woodward climbed down and went around to the rear of the funeral coach and opened the doors. He and Seth lifted out Martin's coffin and laid it on the boards; then Hank took two lariats from the hearse and coiled one at each end of the coffin.

Afterwards, they took the second coffin to the freshly dug grave roughly forty yards down the road, and put it on the boards across the grave. At the back corner of the cemetery was a weathered tool-shed. Woodward tied his team to a hitching post there, and as he walked back towards Martin's grave, he saw the minister drive through the gate in a livery buggy.

As the preacher came toward them, Woodward took out a watch from his vest pocket and saw that it lacked a few minutes of being ten-thirty. More people than just the preacher should be here by now, he thought.

The minister, in frock coat and black hat, was fat, middle-aged and passably clean. Yesterday had been the day of his weekly shave.

"How do you feel today, Dave? Full of wind, wisdom and words?" Woodward asked. He didn't like the Reverend Dave Harper and seldom bothered to hide it. Harper was a loud and illiterate member of some strange, hell-and-brimstone splinter sect that annoyed Hank. He specialized in windy funeral orations.

"Yes, words of commiseration," the Reverend Harper said.

"Well, cut them short today," Hank said. "There's another funeral in half an hour. Are you leading him up to the pearly gates too?"

"No, this is my only funeral today."

"You talk as if sometimes you had more than one," Hank gibed.

"I've been known to have," the Reverend

Harper said with dignity.

"How could you stand yourself?"

"You are addressing a man of the cloth, Mr. Woodward."

"I certainly am, and I'm telling you to make it short and sweet. No, it's not necessary to make it sweet just short."

Again Woodward looked at his watch. It was minutes past the half-hour and there was not a person in sight save the sexton and the preacher.

But now the sound of many horses came to them and they looked over at the gate in time to see the Triangle H crew, numbering about fifteen, ride in at a trot. Will-John Seton, minus his arm sling, headed the crew and led them directly down the tree-lined road. Will-John reined his horse in and looked at the waiting group before dismounting. Behind him the members of the crew dismounted too. At a signal from Will-John, they moved up toward the open grave leading their horses. They spilled off the road onto old graves and the Reverend Harper looked at them disapprovingly before he said to Will-John, "Your men are trampling graves, Mr. Seton."

"Nobody can feel them do it, can they, preacher?" Will-John watched until his crew had formed a loose circle around the grave, then he took off his hat, the crew members removed theirs and Will-John said, "Get going, Dave."

The minister stepped forward to the foot of the coffin, removed his black hat, bowed his head and began a prayer. It was a rambling, windy thing, and Hank Woodward let it run on for ten minutes before be loudly cleared his throat. The Reverend Harper managed to wind it up in another minute. Afterwards he took a slip of paper from his pocket glanced at it to make sure he had the name right and then consigned the soul of Joseph Martin to his Maker.

As he was doing so, a hundred yards behind him, across the cemetery, the first two riders of a dozen came through the gate. They turned right on one of the cemetery lanes, reached the side road that bordered the cemetery and turned onto the road where both graves were open. The Triangle H riders who were facing in that direction exchanged glances, but were silent. They watched Hank and the sexton each slip a loop of the lariat over the ends of the pine box. Hank said, "Will somebody please pull these boards out from under. All right Seth, heave."

They lifted up the coffin and one of the Triangle H crew came forward and pulled the boards out and the coffin was lowered.

It was at this juncture that Jim Donovan

rode in quietly and went up to the group, dismounted, took off his hat and stood beside his horse. The preacher stepped forward, scooped up a handful of earth, and went through the litany of man beginning as dust and turning to dust. His handful of earth fell almost silently on the coffin, and the ceremony was over.

Jim was already moving, leading his horse around the group to place himself between Triangle H and the group of dismounted nesters down the road. Will-John, hat on again, was busy paying the preacher, and as he was doing so a Triangle H hand spoke quietly to him.

"I know they're there," he said to the man. "Do you think I'm deaf?" The transaction was finished as the sexton dropped into the grave on top of the coffin, retrieved the lariats and climbed out. Hank Woodward joined him and they pushed between the Triangle H horses and past Jim, heading for the second funeral. Jim watched the dismounted nesters standing in much the same attitude as the Triangle H group had a few moments ago. The Triangle H crew waited Will-John's signal to mount; but Will-John leading his horse, moved over to Jim and halted beside him.

"I heard the news," Jim said pleasantly. "Congratulations."

"Thanks," Will-John said absently. He was looking at the nesters.

To make casual conversation, Jim said, "Quick marriages are getting to be a Hethridge habit, seems like."

Will-John smiled faintly and looked at him. "After Saturday night, I figured we might as well get married while I was still alive."

"You planning on not being?"

Will-John said wryly, "I walked into that ambush. It was a mistake. I won't have to make one today. The ducks are on the pond." He lifted his arm and pointed to the nesters.

"You're on the same pond, Will-John. Don't do it."

"It's about even. I like the odds." He turned to mount.

Then Will-John halted and looked at Jim with a frown. A look of amazement slowly came into his face and he moved back to Jim. "So help me. I don't think you know. Where you been sleepin' the last couple of nights?"

"The River House."

"Not D Cross?"

"No. Why?"

"And nobody's told you?"

"What?"

"Why, the nesters burned you out. There's nothin' standin' at your place, nothin'."

Jim tried to look surprised and shocked and disbelieving. "Who told you that?"

"Old Parker told one of the hands. We all

208

know it." He snorted softly. "You ought to be leadin' this bunch instead of me. You're the one that's hurt." He paused, and then asked curiously, "What does it take to make you mad?"

Jim reached into his shirt pocket, lifted out the deputy's badge and showed it to Will-John. "A lot when I'm packing this."

Will-John didn't bother to look surprised, and instinctively Jim knew that Harry Andrews had told him of his new deputy. If that was so, if he had seen Will-John before the funeral, it meant that Will-John had told Andrews to stay away, and now he put this thought in words. "I thought somebody representing the law should show up here, Will-John. That's because I think you told Harry and his two deputies to stay away. Did you tell Hank Woodward to hold the two funerals together too?"

Will-John said quietly, matter-of-factly, "No. I asked him when he was burying Shorty Linder. When he told me eleven, I said we'd be burying Joe at ten-thirty. Now stay out of it, Jim. You asked out and I said yes."

He started to mount, but Jim said sharply, "Stay here, Will-John, while I go talk to the nesters."

Will-John looked at him levelly, "They'll kill you. They're burying a man you shot."

"So they are," Jim said, and he stepped into the saddle, put his horse in motion and rode slowly down the lane toward the group of nesters. He was halfway there before he became aware of the sound of horses being walked behind him. He turned in the saddle and saw that Will-John had given the order to mount and that the Triangle H crew, singly and in pairs were following close to Will-John's horse, which was following him. He felt a swift anger, combined with a feeling of outraged helplessness. Will-John was determined to make it appear that he was linked with Triangle H.

As he reached the nesters' group, Hank Woodward and Seth Miller were slipping the lariats around the ends of Shorty Linder's coffin. Jim looked at the nesters then. He knew all the malcontents and their rumored leaders. He saw the hostility and apprehension in those men's faces and noted that to a man they were armed.

He reined in and dismounted and asked the group, "You men got a preacher coming?"

They looked at him and past him at the approaching Triangle H crew.

"No," somebody said.

"You want one? There's Dave Harper heading for his buggy." He tilted his head toward the preacher, who had skirted the Triangle H crew and was going for his buggy.

Hank Woodward said, "They don't want one, Jim. They told me so."

"Then let's get on with the service, if everyone's here."

"You *tellin'* us?" Arly Green asked angrily. He was standing beside his ground-haltered horse, a gaunt elbow resting on the saddle, his hand within easy reach of the rifle in the saddle scabbard.

"You could call it that. This is a Pauper's grave, Arly. County land. I work for the county, so I guess I'm telling you. Hold whatever ceremony you want, bury him and leave."

"Since when did you work for the county?"

"Since this morning." Jim reached in his pocket, took out his badge and showed them. The Triangle H crew was halted in the road, listening and watching.

There was a long silence and then Arly said, "Well, by God! A sheriff and three deputies in this county, and all of 'em workin' for Triangle H."

"Not me, Arly. Ask Will-John."

"He don't belong to us," Will-John said.

Arly looked at the other nesters, then at Will-John, "Then outside of us, he's the only thing that don't belong to you in this county." He straightened up and his huge hands fell to his side. Looking at Jim he said, "We're all Irish here, Donovan. We're aimin' to hold a wake before we bury Shorty."

Jim knew he was being baited, knew that the memory of the Saturday night fight and the two deaths made every man here edgy. He also knew that the nesters had been drinking, Arly in particular, and that they, like Will-John, welcomed this spot as a field of battle. And he further knew that some bold and decisive move on his part was necessary before this blew up.

"It's too late for the wake, Arly." He moved past Hank and the coffin and approached Arly and stopped in front of him. "Remember the way you came in. Go out the same way. I'll see Shorty's buried. Do that, or you're under arrest."

"You'll see him buried!" Arly shouted. "Hell, you killed him!"

His big hand drove for his gun and Jim lunged at him. Arly's gun was half out of its holster when Jim drove a shoulder into his chest, at the same time clamping his left hand on Arly's wrist. Arly lost his balance and slammed back into his horse. There was a shot then Arly's horse reared and fell over backwards screaming in pain.

Jim hit the ground on top of Arly and then pandemonium broke loose. Some of the nesters tried to mount, and Jim heard Will-John shout, "Ride 'em down!"

Jim, with his hands still clamped on Arly's wrist, placed his forearm on Arly's throat and bent his head back. He could hear the sound of galloping horses and of a wild shouting and shooting on all sides of him.

He brought his knee up into Arly's groin, and Arly released the butt of his gun. Then Jim dug in a boot toe which gave him purchase and slugged at Arly's unshaven jaw. After the second blow he felt Arly go limp. As he was rising to look round him, a horse bowled him over on top of Arly.

Lying there on his belly, Jim looked around. Hank Woodward was crouched down beside the coffin. All over the cemetery there was shooting, rider following rider in pursuit, through the trees and over the gaves. Jim saw one rider try to jump his horse over a wrought-iron grave fence. The horse slipped and impaled itself in the spikes, and shrieked and fought and threw its rider, then galloped off, limping. There was the steady fire of shooting and Jim saw that the team pulling the hearse had broken loose and was dragging the hearse across the cemetery. It careened wildly as it hit a tombstone and then turned on its side.

Will-John, Jim saw, was in a shooting pursuit of a rider just going trough the gate. The firing was becoming more distant now. Jim knew that Triangle H had succeeded in putting the nesters to rout.

Coming erect, he surveyed the carnage among the trees. He could count three downed horses, two of them with riders pinned under them. The rider of the third downed horse sat propped up against a tombstone, arms wrapped around his belly. One Triangle H rider lay on his back in the road, apparently the victim of the opening fusillade.

Hank Woodward, his black suit dusty, joined Jim as he stood looking down at Arly. "Good God, what a fight!" Hank said, his voice shaking with fright. "You could have stopped it, Jim."

"Who scheduled these funerals half an hour apart, Hank? Not me."

"I had to get the bodies underground in this weather," Hank protested.

Jim said grimly, "From the looks of this you'll have to get some more underground."

At his feet Arly stirred now, sat up and shook his head.

"What do we do now, Jim?" Hank asked helplessly.

"Why, your sexton is hiding over by the shed, Hank. With Arly helping, the three of us can get the hearse right side up. If anybody's alive, take them to the doctor in that. Now, on your feet, Arly. You've got work to do, and then a long walk to town."

15

That Monday morning, after Doc Purcell was finished with his house calls, he examined Keefe Hart and released him from the two-bed hospital in his home. Hart had to carry his hat in his left hand because his head was bandaged and so was his right hand. His progress toward River Street was painfully slow. There was no way to hide his bruised and discolored face, so when the people he met on the slow journey looked shocked at his appearance, he eyed them defiantly with his malevolent pale eyes. When he arrived at the First Chance, he found it open, but empty of everyone save Tim O'Guy. Moving slowly toward the bar, Hart waited until O'Guy came up to him, then said, "A water glass of whiskey, Tim."

"You don't look too bad," O'Guy observed. "They told me you was wrecked."

"Who's seen me beside the Doc?" Hart asked wryly, putting his hat on the bar.

"Why, everybody thought you was too sick to visit."

"Or not worth it, because I was too crippled to fight?"

O'Guy read his temper, took a bottle of whiskey and a glass from underneath the bar and set them before Hart. The lean Texan poured himself a glassful of whiskey, and took three quick drafts of it as if it were beer.

When he got his breath back, he said, "My gear still upstairs?" At Tim's nod he said, "Rifle and saddle too?"

"Everything you left."

"Where is everybody?"

"Burying Shorty Linder. You knew they got him, didn't you?"

"Yeah, Doc told me. Seton been in again?"

"Not since you doused him."

"When he comes in you let me know," Hart said, and he added, "Don't worry, I'll take the fight out in the street."

He finished his whiskey and awkwardly pulled out some money with his left hand, turned the glass upside down over the bottle, took the bottle and headed toward the back of the room, where a railed stairway went up to the loft.

The single room above that he entered ran the length of the building, with a window in front and a window at the rear. Although they were both open, the air was stifling. Along the side wall, jutting out into the room, were per-

217

haps ten blanketed cots. On some of the cots were warbags of other transient owners. Hart's cot was closest to the front window, and he saw his saddle and rifle and warbag on it, just as Tim O'Guy said he would.

The walk here and the climb up the stairs had exhausted Hart. He lifted the saddle and warbag and put them on the floor at the foot of the cot and then put the bottle of whiskey and the glass on the floor beside the cot, and lay down. He suddenly remembered he had left his hat at the bar downstairs, but O'Guy would take care of that.

In these past few days, he had had plenty of time to think. The deal he had made with the nesters was probably off. He thought they would consider him incapable of delivering what he had promised, namely the killing of Will-John Seton. Far from having any confidence in him now, they probably held him in contempt for letting Will-John give him the beating he had taken.

Hart was momentarily distracted by what he thought was the sound of distant gunfire. It was so faint, however, he could not be sure. Probably some puncher was getting married and he and his bride were being given a send-off. This interruption, however, did not alter the course of his reflections. In a day or two, when he had his strength back and was able to travel, he knew what he was going to do. He had given much thought to the layout of Triangle H, dredging his memory for every last detail of that fateful Friday afternoon. He remembered the approach below the lake where the stream was screened by big alders. It would not be difficult to reach there at night and fort up. He could keep the house, bunkhouse and office under observation. It might take days before he got a chance at Will-John Seton, but with that good cover and enough food, he could wait him out. Will-John would not be on the alert for an ambush, since he likely thought Hart had drifted, a normal enough thing to do after such a beating.

The problem of a horse bothered Hart, but not too much. He could rent a livery rig to get out there, turn the horse loose and it would go back to its familiar feed stable. His getaway horse was another matter. He'd have to take Will-John's horse, and there was always the danger that the horse would spook and leave him afoot at the mercy of whoever came to investigate the sound of the shooting. He would have to trust to luck on that, but he mustn't trust to luck on his marksmanship. He would use his carbine, of course, for the job, but he would have to shoot it left-handed, since his right hand was useless.

He sat up now and poured himself another drink of whiskey, then picked up his carbine. For the next half-hour he practiced sighting on the rafter nails at the far end of the room. Once the strangeness wore off, and he learned to close his right eye instead of his left the business didn't seem too awkward. Tomorrow he'd ride out of town and practice with live ammunition. When he was sure he could hit a moving target with any precision, he would be ready for the job.

Maybe because of the whiskey, he felt the deepest sort of exhaustion. He lay back, and in seconds was engulfed by sleep.

Sometime later he was dragged from his deep sleep by a commotion downstairs and the excited shouts of men's voices. He was drowsily speculating on what it meant when a man pounded up the stairs, taking them two at a time. Rifle in hand, he ran the length of the building and peered out of the window. There was shouting out in the street now and Hart came up on his elbows.

"What the hell's happening?" he asked.

The man, who had not seen him, turned his head to look at him. "Gun fight at the cemetery."

"Who?"

"Us and the Triangle H crew."

Now shooting started out in the street and

was answered by gunfire from downstairs.

Hart swung his legs off the bed, took some shells from his shell belt lying on the blanket, and hastily loaded his carbine. The man at the window raised his gun, shot, then ducked back.

Hart moved over past the man to the right side of the window, but before he could look out his attention was diverted by a thuderous racket downstairs.

"They're tryin' to break in," the man said.

Hart didn't answer. He edged half his head past the window frame and had a look at the street. The Triangle H crew had left their horses in the middle of the street, and Hart guessed the number of mounts at ten. The riders were out of sight but apparently close to the saloon. Now the battering below seemed to be at both front and back doors, and through the racket came the sound of shouting. Hart was about to draw back when he saw a man who had been crouched behind one of the horses come erect. The man looked at the building and then took the trailing reins of the horse he had hidden behind and led it alongside another horse, whose reins he also picked up.

There was something familiar about this man, and Hart now moved square into the window and had a good look. It came to him

221

then that this man was one of the three who had witnessed his beating out at Triangle H, the slight blond-haired one. Cursing softly, Hart levered a shell into his carbine chamber and brought the rifle to his left shoulder. He remembered his practice and was careful to keep his left eye open as he drew down on the man in the street. He watched until the man took the trailing reins of yet another horse and stood looking at what was going on below. Carefully, Hart drew in a breath and held it centered on the man's chest and gently squeezed the trigger.

The man's hat flew off and he was half turned by the impact of the bullet; then he fell on his back in the dust of the street.

"Got him," Hart said quietly.

The other man came up beside him and looked out at the man in the street. Then he said softly, "Oh, Jesus. That's Cole Hethridge. Let's get out of here."

They both turned and saw, for the first time, the fire rising out of the stairwell. While they'd been watching the street and shooting, the building had been set afire.

Both Hart and the other man had taken less than ten steps toward the stairs when the kerosene-soaked landing blossomed into orange flame.

Hart's companion ran toward the flames,

and Hart, cursing his own slowness, hobbled after him.

The flames at the head of the stairs were knee-high by now, and the puncher, holding his arm against his mouth, walked into them in a determined effort to break for his freedom. He had taken only one step down the stairs when the fire of the blazing stairwell stopped him. The wood was already crackling, and the flames, started by the coal oil and fed by the upward draft of air from below, filled the stairwell.

He turned and ran back, slapping at the flames that had set his pants afire and were reaching his shirt.

Smoke was pouring up out of the stairwell, lifting to the ridge pole and spreading. The man halted by Hart. "No way out there, feller," he said in a choked voice.

"The back window."

"You'd be on fire before you'd make it. It's got to be the street window." They listened to the shooting downstairs and the man said, "Quick. Maybe they're all inside."

He ran past Hart to the street window and looked out, then he hoisted himself to the sill, put both legs over, turned his upper body, gripped the sill with both hands and lowered himself. His head was disappearing when the shot came. Head and hands disappeared, and

Hart moved up to one side of the window. Looking down, he could see the man's sprawled legs on the boardwalk. The rest of his body was cut off from view.

Hart drew back and looked down the room. The other end of the room was a sheet of fire, and Hart knew he could not make it through the flames to the back window. Besides, they would be waiting at the back window too.

The smoke was becoming thicker, and Hart squatted down beside the front window where the air was cleaner. Maybe, just maybe, he thought desperately, whoever had shot his companion would think he had got the only man upstairs. After all, Triangle H did not know he had left Doc Purcell's hospital and come here. The thing to do, then, was to wait until the fire drove him out, hoping that in those few minutes of grace their attention would be drawn elsewhere.

From the sounds of the firing below it seemed as if the fight had moved toward the back door. Hart stood up and, widely skirting the window, he came to his cot. He threw his carbine on it, took out his pistol and checked its loads, and then, choking on the smoke, he went back to the window and again hunkered down on his heels.

For a moment he allowed himself to wonder why he had let himself be tolled into this country. He knew Triangle H's old reputation for vengefulness and he had been a fool to come.

But now he heard from down the street the loud clanging of iron on iron. That, he knew, would be the summons to the volunteer fire department. If he could hold out a few more minutes it would allow time for the fire fighters to arrive. The Triangle H crew would be afraid to gun him down in front of all the witnesses who would be watching.

The fire, he saw, was spreading rapidly, and now the burning blankets on the cots added their acrid smoke to the woodsmoke. The draft from the stairwell and the open window at the rear of the room drove the flames toward him in a surging wave. The roof had caught fire now and two-thirds of the room was ablaze. The heat was almost unbearable.

Hart decided that the moment had come, and he stood up again by the window and put a leg over the sill. He had the other leg lifted to swing it out when the shot came from the street. It got him in his right shoulder with a slam that drove him back into the room and sprawled him on the floor.

He lay there on his belly, head toward the fire. He knew that in moments the fire would reach him. Well, he was not going that way. He crawled back to the wall and the movement brought the pain to his shattered shoulder.

Get it over with, he thought. He hauled himself to his feet, gun in hand, and moved openly into the window frame. Standing there, choking from the smoke billowing around him, eyes watering, he sought a target down on the street. Men were running, and he could not tell friend from enemy.

What's it matter? he thought savagely, and raised his gun to shoot at a man running.

That was when the enemy found him. He heard the first shot, but his own cry of anguish drowned the second shot, which killed him.

16

The hearse holding three wounded men and Arly Green, had just cleared the cemetery gates when Jim picked up the distant sound of gunfire. It came from town and Jim knew that the running fight was continuing.

For an uncertain moment he wondered if he should abandon Arly and hurry into town, and then reason prevailed. Arly was his prisoner, arrested, not because he had gone for his gun, but because Jim wanted to question him about the nesters and the burning of D Cross. That was why he had asked to be deputized, not to head off the battle between Triangle H and the nesters. He had done his best to halt that, so now let the sheriff and his two deputies take care of it.

Arly, sitting on the hearse floor facing Jim, legs trailing down, held the hearse doors open as Hank Woodward tried to get some speed out of the team. The shooting in town continued, and Jim knew with a grim certainty that either Sheriff Andrews had made himself

scarce, or that if he was in town he was power-
less to stop the fighting.

At Doc Purcell's white frame house, the
hearse pulled up. Jim dismounted and ordered
Arly to take the legs of one of the wounded
men while he himself took the shoulders. He
didn't want Arly out of his sight.

Mrs. Purcell, who had probably watched
them through the window, opened the door
for them and indicated the blanket which she
had spread out on the parlor floor. As they
went out, Hal and the sexton came up the
walk carrying the second man. Jim and Arly
carried the third man in. When Jim went out
again, Arly ahead of him, the firing was slack-
ing off. Before he had reached his horse,
he heard the iron clanging of the fire alarm.
Arly turned and said over his shoulder, "That
means there's a fire, don't it?"

Jim nodded. "One you won't see. Head for
the courthouse, Arly."

As they reached the courthouse, the firing
had stopped entirely except for the last two
isolated rifle shots.

In the courthouse Jim found the door to the
sheriff's office open, but neither Andrews nor
his two deputies were there.

"Sit there," Jim said, indicating the straight-
back chair by the desk, and Arly shambled
over to it and sat down. Jim took Arly's gun

from his waistband, tossed it and his hat on the desk, and then slacked into the sheriff's chair.

Looking at Arly, Jim thought he had sobered up, although he still stank of moonshine. "Well, Arly," he began, "you got what you wanted, didn't you? Four dead men out there and God knows how many more in town."

"You started it," Arly said sullenly.

"If you'd come along peaceably, it might not have happened. But you had to go for your gun. That'll be proven by witnesses at your second trial — if there is a second trial."

Arly fixed a glance from bloodshot eyes on him. Above the collar of his filthy shirt, Jim saw his Adam's apple bob in the act of swallowing. "Second trial?" Arly said slowly. "What's the first for?"

"Conspiracy to murder Joe Martin. Attempted murder of Will-John Seton and of me."

"I tell you I wasn't in that bunch Saturday night!"

"You're lying, Arly. And if you keep on lying, you're a plain fool. Know why?"

Arly moved his head from side to side, signifying that he didn't.

"Because if you're convicted on that charge, Arly, they can hang you. On this second charge of resisting arrest out at the cemetery, they can't hang you if you're convicted."

There was a long pause as Arly pondered this. "What you getting at?"

"This, Arly. If you give us the truth on what happened Saturday night, we'll ask the Judge to be lenient in his sentence after your trial. I'll even request the District Attorney to drop charges of resisting arrest. So you won't be tried a second time."

"And what if I tell you nothin'?"

"Then we'll ask the D. A. to push for your hanging. If you get off with a long prison sentence, we'll push for your second trial. That'll add a little time to the sentence you'll have already got."

"You can't prove a damn thing!" Arly said.

"Well, you'll have plenty of time to think it over in the jail downstairs, Arly. Just so you remember what I said." He paused and regarded Arly carefully. "Tell me what I said, Arly. Are you sober enough to remember it?"

"I'm sober," Arly said angrily. "You told me if I'd help you on that Saturday night ruckus, you'd ask the Judge to go easy. If I didn't, you'll ask him to hang me. If they don't, you'll try me for today."

"That's it." Jim rose and walked over to the door, looking over his shoulder at Arly as he did so. He reached behind the door for the cell keys and said, "Come along."

Arly rose, and then in one swift movement lunged for the gun on the desk.

Jim's hand streaked for his own gun. "Want it in the back, Arly?" he asked flatly.

Arly froze, then turned and saw Jim's gun leveled at him.

"Stand away from it," Jim said. Arly took two steps toward the door and paused.

"You're doing pretty good, Arly. I figured you'd try that. You just added a third charge. Attempted escape. Now, come along."

Jim waited until Arly was out in the hall, then he came up to the door opposite the sheriff's office and said, "Stand away, Arly."

With his gun in his left hand, he unlocked the door, swung it wide and motioned with his gun for Arly to go down the stairs.

In the three-cell block below, Jim again told him to stand aside; then he unlocked the cell door and motioned with his gun for Arly to step inside. Jim was turning away when Arly said, "When do I get out of here?"

"Why, murder isn't a bailable offense, Arly. You'll stay here until you're tried."

"When'll that be?"

"When the Judge sets the trial date we'll let you know."

Upstairs, Jim hung up the cell keys and put Arly's gun in the desk, then he went out into the corridor, leaving the door unlocked. Instead of going out of the rear door, he moved down the corridor, intending to find out where the fire was. The neighboring office was empty, as were all the others down the length of the corridor. A town fire was something to be feared, and he knew that all available men would answer the alarm.

Outside, he went back to get his horse, mounted and headed down Bridge Street for River Street. As soon as he had turned the corner and could look down River Street, he saw the crowd. The First Chance saloon was ablaze, the crackling flames mounting skyward, and a column of grey-blue smoke towering above them. Coming closer, he saw the pump cart's hose trailing across the street into the river. The stream that was being pumped was aimed, not at the fire, but at the buildings on either side of the First Chance. If the fire could be prevented from spreading the town was safe. The First Chance, of course, was gone.

Leaving his horse at the River House tie rail, he walked toward the fire. He saw Kate on the edge of the crowd in the middle of the road and went up to her. When he halted beside her, she turned her head and an expression of wild relief came to her face.

"Oh, Jim, you're all right! Nobody knew

anything except that you were in the cemetery fight."

"I was on the ground and on top of Arly Green. Maybe they thought they'd already got me. What happened here?"

Kate answered with open bitterness. "The nesters tried to hole up in O'Guy's place, so Will-John's men burned it down. Cole Hethridge was killed right here in the street." She asked vehemently then: "What's happened to these men, Jim? They're like two packs of mad dogs!"

Jim nodded, his face grim. "I'm glad Burt Hethridge isn't here to see the end of what he started. Does Sarah know about Cole?"

"Yes, she knows. When the shooting was over she came to the fire and someone told her. She started over to see him. Will-John tried to stop her, but she went anyway. She looked at him and didn't shed a tear. Will-John took her to the River House." Kate looked at Jim and he saw the tears in her eyes. "Isn't that a wonderful wedding present? Your brother killed on your wedding day? They even say the man who killed Cole is still in that building, Jim. My God, what have we come to? We're animals! We're animals even for watching it."

"Is Harry Andrews here?"

"Yes," Kate said with contempt. "He came

on the scene when it was all over. The nesters fought their way out and ran. The sheriff sent the Triangle H crew out of town. Two of them were hit. There are two more dead men lying out there under the tarp alongside Cole. Nobody knows if there are other men in that fire. Where were you, Jim?"

Jim told her of taking the wounded from the cemetery to Doc Purcell's and of locking up the prisoner. He finished up by saying, "You look like hell, Kate. Go back to your office and away from this."

Kate nodded and said, "Will you stop by?"

Jim said he would, and then he pushed through the crowd. As he broke into a cleared space around the First Chance, the floor of the second story collapsed with a muffled crash, bulging the sides of the burning building. Lying in the middle of the street, in a bay formed by the crowd, was the body of Cole and the two others, their boots, toes pointed skywards, jutting out beyond the edge of the covering tarp.

Looking in the other direction, Jim saw Harry Andrews talking to his two slack-jawed nephew-deputies. As Jim went over toward him, the two nephews nodded and then turned and vanished in the crowd. Jim came up to the sheriff and halted before him. They could feel the heat of the burning building now. The sheriff, his face harried and bewildered, pointed with a thrust of his chin to the hose cart, where four men were pumping the handles that shot the stream of water on the building next door. "Looks like they got it wet enough. The boys have gone for a wagon to haul the bodies away. Nothing we can do here, Jim. Let's go back to the office."

Jim had his mouth open to say he had just come from the office, but he refrained. There were a lot of questions he wanted to ask Harry Andrews, but this was hardly the place to ask them. Together, they pushed through the crowd and parted, each heading for his horse. Mounted, they joined in the middle of the next block, riding side by side. "Ever hear of anything like this?" the sheriff asked.

"No."

Jim's tone of voice, from which he could not keep his anger, made the sheriff turn his head and look at him. Jim didn't return his glance and they rode the rest of the way to the courthouse in silence. Dismounting at the tie rail there, Jim headed for the sheriff's office, while the sheriff rode on to the open shed behind the courthouse, where he stalled his horse. In the sheriff's office Jim did not sit down, but restlessly prowled the room until the sheriff came in and went to his desk, where he took off his hat and slacked into his swivel chair.

"My God, what do we do now?" the sheriff said in a whining voice.

Jim stopped. "We clear up a few things first, Harry. Why weren't you and your deputies at the cemetery?"

"Why, we was busy. I didn't know about the funerals today. Neither did the boys. Besides, I don't go to funerals."

"You knew about the funerals, Harry."

"Why do you think I knew? I said I didn't."

Jim walked over to face him, halted, and rammed his hands in his hip pockets. "Before the fight started, I showed Will-John my badge. He wasn't surprised. He knew I had it. How did he know?"

"Why, I told him."

"Did you talk about the funerals?"

"Well, he said they were burying Joe Martin this morning."

"And for you to stay away from the cemetery?" Jim asked

"Nobody tells me to stay away from anywhere," the sheriff said angrily.

"Answer my question, Harry. Did he tell you to keep away from the cemetery?"

The sheriff's face was flushed. "Well, he did say he wouldn't need me out there. Besides, you was out there, I hear."

"But not on your orders, Harry. You know

what happened out there?"

"A fight, they tell me."

"Four men killed and three men hurt. I tried to stop it and couldn't."

"You think I could have?" the sheriff asked bitterly.

"I think four of us would have had a better chance of stopping it than I had alone," Jim said flatly.

"How could I have guessed what would happen?"

"You knew what would happen," Jim said sharply. "You stayed away so it would happen. Where were you when the fight moved to the First Chance?"

"Why, I was on my way out to Beau Cather's to ask him about Saturday's fight. Like you said I should. I heard the shooting from a long ways off and I came back as quick as I could. It was all over when I got here."

"Yes. I'll bet you made sure of that, Harry."

Jim made a slow circle of the room, hands still in his hip pockets. The sheriff watched him, his pale eyes bright with hatred. Jim made a full circle and halted in the same spot before the sheriff.

"What are you going to do now?"

The sheriff slowly lifted his hand to his badge, unpinned it and threw it on the desk. "Resign."

Jim said contemptuously, "That's the way to face up to it, Harry. I suppose your nephews will face up to it the same way."

"They won't work for anybody but me, so I reckon they will." He added with sly satisfaction, "That leaves you, don't it?"

Jim nodded. "I don't know how legal it is to serve under a sheriff who's resigned, but I'll find out. Now I'm going to make my first arrest, Harry."

"Who?"

"You."

Jim pulled his gun out, leaned over and lifted the sheriff's gun from it's holster.

Andrews, stunned by Jim's move, made no effort to stop him. Jim rammed the sheriff's gun in his belt, holstered his own and stepped back.

The sheriff said, "My resignation ain't taken effect yet."

"Turn around and write it out," Jim said.

"Not with a gun on me."

"There's no gun on you. I'll even leave the room while you write it. If you're bluffing, Harry, I'm calling your bluff. I'll even take your resignation to the chairman of the Board of Commissioners. You won't have to face them."

The sheriff sat undecided for a long moment. Jim guessed what he was thinking: he intended to resign right enough, but he preferred to do it in his own way. Still, not having to face the Commissioners and their angry accusations appealed to the coward in him. There would be words between him and the Commissioners eventually, but he would not have to face their initial wrath.

He swiveled his chair to face the desk, drew out a piece of paper from the cubbyhole and penciled his brief note of resignation, which he held out to Jim.

Jim read it and was pocketing it when Andrews asked, "What charges are you arresting me on?"

"Dereliction of office. After I talk with Judge Conover I'll have others." He paused, isolating what he was about to say. "You see, Harry, you're the one to blame for this massacre today. Only you and your office could have stopped it. Instead, you turned tail and ran. I don't have to tell you that's a violation of your oath of office."

The sheriff's voice was thick with anger as he said, "If I've resigned my office, I've resigned yours too. I appointed you, and now I fire you. You can't arrest even a town drunk."

"Harry, there's a thing called a citizen's arrest that goes back to English common law. If a man sees a crime being committed the law gives him the power to arrest the criminal.

You're the criminal, Harry. Now stand up and I'll put you in your jail."

Wordlessly, Sheriff Andrews rose and, without waiting for Jim, opened the stair doors and descended.

17

It was mid-afternoon of that bright day of blood-lust when Will-John and Sarah, in a rented buggy, drove into Triangle H. The guard was stationed at the point where the road began to swing around the lake, and Will-John asked him if both crews were here. The man told him they were. Only then did he ask the guard, "Does Mrs. Hethridge know about Cole?"

"They told her." He touched his hat and looked at Sarah. "Sorry about that, ma'am. We all are."

Sarah, her face as still and expressionless as the calm lake she was watching, only nodded.

Although Will-John was impatient to talk with the crew of Number Two, he drove the buggy to the Big House gate. He had no idea how the two women would react to their mutual loss when they met, but he made a bet with himself. Sarah had had her cry. It was a short one, and he suspected it was more out of ritual sentiment than true grief. He had not watched Sarah all these years without learning something about her. The affection between Cole and Sarah had died at the end of their childhood, and after that they had held only antagonistic toleration for each other. As for Bonnie, that was easy. She wouldn't bother feigning grief to him, but maybe she would to Sarah. She had what she wanted now, which was half of Triangle H, and Cole's death would mean to her only the removal of a nuisance. He hoped she wouldn't show that feeling to Sarah.

He handed Sarah down from the buggy just as Bonnie stepped out on the porch. Will-John opened the gate for Sarah, then took off his hat and let her precede him up the walk. She went up the steps and the two women embraced; both of them were crying, as befitted the occasion. They clung to each other for a moment and then drew apart.

Will-John, his face grave, held out his hand to Bonnie. "It was over quick for him, Mrs. Hethridge. He never knew it happened."

Bonnie wiped tears from her eyes and said, "They told me that. They also told me that you and Sarah were married this morning. It's a sad day for good wishes, but you have mine."

"I think Sarah would like to rest if she can," Will-John said. "I reckon you would too."

Bonnie nodded and put her arm through

Sarah's, and they moved into the house. Will-John went out to the buggy, lifted out Sarah's valise and set it on the porch. Then he drove the buggy back to the office tie rail. He and Sarah had agreed they would stay at the Big House till they could assess the results of this day's happenings.

When Will-John reached the tie rail some of the crew who had been lounging in the bunkhouse doorway came to meet him.

"Everybody here?" Will-John asked, as he wound the reins around the whip stock.

He was told they were, and he went into the bunkhouse, followed by the half-dozen men who had met him.

In the cool dim-lit interior he saw that he had interrupted a game of poker at the big table.

"Who's hurt?" he asked first.

"Ben Berry and Goose Evans," Les said. "Not bad though." He gestured over his shoulder with a thumb. "They're in the end bunks."

Will-John went over and talked to the men, asking about their injuries and what they had done to take care of them. After that he walked back to the table, where the poker game had been discontinued.

Will-John shoved the pile of poker chips aside and sat on the end of the table, his legs dangling. Slowly, the men of both crews drifted to seats on the bunks, both upper and lower, so they could face him.

When they were settled Will-John asked, "How many we missing, Les, besides Cole?"

"Three." Les named them, and added, "I stopped by the cemetery. They lost four there and three in town. They had some hurt, too."

Will-John stroked his jaw in thoughtful silence. The figures he heard spoke for themselves. Triangle H had won the fight, the nesters were routed, their hangout burned to the ground. Condolences for their own dead weren't in order, for Triangle H was a fighting outfit; every man here had hired on with the assurance his job was rough and risky, take it or leave it.

Finally Will-John said, "Bill, how'd it go with you?"

Bill Costigan, ramrod for Number Two, was an emaciated, quiet-spoken man in his fifties who smelled of saddle leather and horses, a man who lived in the saddle and would sooner be caught naked than walking across even a narrow street.

Bill took the brown cigarette from the corner of his mouth and said, "No trouble. We burned Shorty Linder's place so nobody'd move into it. Arly Green wasn't there and we burned his. Beau Cather was in that Saturday

244

night ruckus. He's gut-shot and he'll die. We put him outside under a tree and burned him out. He was out of his head and didn't know us. Davy Forsyth saw us comin' and ran. He had some powder in his shack, so we got some fireworks. Prewitt wasn't about to fight, so his place went up." He paused, ruminating, then added, "That's about it, Will-John. Not a shot fired."

"You think that's enough of 'em?"

"It's all we had time for, seein's you wanted us back here by noon. If it ain't enough, we can hit more of 'em."

Will-John thought a moment. "No, I reckon you got the ones we wanted most. Remember, there's four at the cemetery we don't have to burn out."

"What's goin' to happen now, Will-John?" Bill asked.

"Not a damn thing," Will-John said flatly. "Who can make anything happen? The Commissioners can go over Andrews' head and ask for a U. S. Marshal. He can't touch us. They jumped me Saturday night and killed one of our men. They started the fight at the cemetery. They made the fight, not us."

There was a murmur of assent from the crew, and Will-John slid off the table. "Number Two crew stays here tonight, Les. Keep your guards out all night. I don't reckon we'll need 'em, but you can't tell what those crazy fools will try."

"There ain't enough of 'em left to try anything," Les said.

"That's what I hope," Will-John said. He waved a casual salute and went out of the bunkhouse. Had he been gone long enough for Sarah to be already having a nap? He thought he had, and he headed for the Big House and it's back door. If Sarah, instead of resting, was talking with Bonnie, he could pretend he had come to give them Bill's news of the successful raids.

Bonnie answered his knock on the kitchen door and stepped aside to let him in. Will-John raised his hand, a finger pointing upstairs.

"She's sleeping," Bonnie said. "Come in."

Will-John stepped inside and took her in his arms and she willingly came against him as they kissed. Bonnie put her arms around him and touched his wounded arm. Will-John flinched and broke away from her, feeling his arm gingerly.

"I almost forgot I had it." He looked closely at her and saw that she was smiling. "You did it on purpose."

She nodded. "That's for marrying that old maid upstairs this morning."

"She tell you all about it?"

246

"It's the greatest thing that ever happened to her. Why wouldn't she?"

Bonnie moved over to the table and sat down. Will-John took off his hat and sat down in the chair opposite her, putting his hat on the table. They studied each other in silence for a moment.

"You feel anything about Cole, Bonnie?"

"Nothing but good."

Will-John frowned. "He wasn't that bad, was he?"

"I didn't mean that." Bonnie absently brushed a wisp of straying black hair back in place. "All along I've been worried about what you said about Cole back in Kansas City. You said you were heading for trouble with these squatters and that an accident would happen to Cole. I thought you meant you'd make it happen, and it worried me. That was our only chance of being caught." She hesitated. "You didn't make it happen, did you, Will-John?"

"No. He was horse-holder out in the street. I gave him that job because he's no damn good in any kind of fight. This Hart that I beat up was upstairs over the saloon. He must have looked out the window and there was Cole. He remembered his beating here, so he shot him."

"Is Triangle H really ours now?"

Will-John smiled and nodded. He reached out and cupped her hands in his. "Sarah says Cole didn't have a will. His half is yours."

"And you'll run Sarah's half and mine?"

"And your money. You'll have all you want, Bonnie."

Bonnie looked searchingly at him. "What I want is you."

"You'll have me. You've still got your shop, haven't you?" At Bonnie's nod, he said, "Then it won't be hard to find you there when you want to be found."

"It's not what you promised me, Will-John."

"No, it isn't. But how could I know then that Sarah would marry me?"

"Why did you ask her again?"

"Why, you nailed down half the outfit when you married Cole. Do I pass up a chance to nail down the other half?" He released her hand and leaned back in his chair. "Bonnie, you've got the world now. Are you sulkin' because there's no red fence around it?"

Bonnie laughed quietly and Will-John knew everything was all right again. It came to him then that Bonnie loved him and was jealous of Sarah. What had begun in cold calculation had ended in this, and Will-John saw the irony of it. He said gently, "You're about as far from the gutter as you can get,

Bonnie. Settle for that."

"But you'll see me?"

"I said I would." He leaned forward and put his arms on the table. "It'll go something like this, Bonnie, depending on you. Can you live in this house with Sarah?"

"Why, of course. I planned to when I married Cole. It's Sarah that won't live in this house with me."

"I think she will. Number Two is way out in the back brush and the house is not what she's used to. With Cole out of here, and with a new husband, she'll change her mind about you. I'll tell her that with Cole gone, I'll have to work out of Triangle H instead of Number Two. We'll be living here in this house with you, Bonnie. Whenever you want me to meet you in town, give me a signal. Wear a certain dress, or close the door to your room, anything. If anybody sees me go into your shop, I've got the best reason in the world for being there. You're half owner of this spread, and I have to talk with you on every move I make."

Bonnie considered this a long moment, and then said, "That sounds almost all right. Almost."

Will-John smiled and stood up. "Bonnie, you've got Mrs. in front of your name, a bank account with no bottom to it, and a man for loving. Forget the red fence."

18

From the Wednesday special edition of the *Banner*:

OUR BLACKEST DAY
Range War Toll Is Eleven Dead
Five Known Injured
Five Ranches Burned

Cole Hethridge Among Those Dead

Jailed Sheriff Resigns Post

The smoldering feud between the Triangle H ranch and the squatters claiming Triangle H range erupted Monday morning in two pitched battles. The first gunfight occurred at the Pitkin cemetery at the grave of Shorty Linder, who was killed in a gunfight Saturday night behind the Masonic Hall. The second fight, a continuation of the first, took place at the First Chance saloon, which was set afire and burned to the ground. This fight claimed the life of Cole Hethridge, who, with his sister, inherited the vast Triangle H properties.

While those fights were taking place, a portion of the big Triangle H crew ravaged the countryside, burning the homes and buildings of five separate ranches.

Sheriff Harry Andrews and his two deputies, Ed and Tam Thatcher, were not present at either of the fights or at any of the burnings. Attorney James Donovan, sworn in as deputy sheriff only an hour before the fight broke out, was present at the cemetery battle and was the only law officer to witness it. Donovan ordered the squatters' group to leave the cemetery and upon their refusal to do so he arrested Arty Green. When Green refused to leave the cemetery and went for his gun, the fighting broke out, resulting in the deaths of seven men.

The absence of any law officers on the scene of the town fight was thought to have made possible this battle and the burning of the First Chance saloon. Deputy Donovan was helping the wounded to Dr. Purcell's hospital when the second fight occurred.

Donovan, in a statement to the *Banner*, said he exercised his right of citizen's arrest to jail Sheriff Andrews. He contended that the sheriff knew that the times of the funerals of Joe Martin, Triangle H hand also killed in Saturday night's ambush, and that of Shorty Linder would overlap, thus bringing the two warring factions together. He further contended that the sheriff was derelict in his duties when he absented himself from the fight in town. Bond was set at $1,000 by Judge Conover and Andrews was released. Also jailed was Arly Green on charges of murder and conspiracy to murder and resisting arrest.

The County Commissioners Monday evening accepted the resignation of Sheriff Andrews, named Donovan acting sheriff and authorized him to request the United States Commissioner in Junction City to dispatch a U. S. Marshal to Pitkin.

The history of the bad feeling between Triangle H and the squatters' group dates back many years to the time when Burt Hethridge owned and operated Triangle H. The squatter group has always maintained they had settled on open range, while Triangle H maintained they were trespassing on already claimed range.

The appalling events of Monday morning were precipitated by the attempted ambush of Will-John Seton, by the squatter faction Saturday night in the alley behind the Masonic Hall. Seton was slightly wounded, and his companion, Joe Martin, was killed, as was Shorty Linder of the squatter faction.

These shameful savageries, climaxed by the burning of the First Chance saloon, obscured the news that Sarah Hethridge, daughter of Burt Hethridge and sister of the dead Cole Hethridge, and Will-John Seton, foreman of Triangle H, were married by Judge Conover early Monday morning.

Funeral services for Cole Hethridge were set for Wednesday at the Community Church at 2 P.M. Services for members of the Triangle H crew will be held at the cemetery at 4 o'clock Wednesday.

Below is a list of the names of those killed and those wounded in Monday's battles. This list is followed by a list of the ranch properties destroyed by fire.

From the editorial page of the same issue:

It was no pleasure for your Editor to record the facts of the lead story on Page One. In fact, it was done with a feeling of revulsion and shame. It is without fear of libeling the former sheriff to say that he let, even encouraged, this festering antagonism between Triangle H and the squatters, till it finally exploded in our faces.

253

And we let him do it.

There has never been any question that Triangle H has abused its great power in this county and others. Like the big company towns in the past that most of us chose to leave, Triangle H made sure it had a local government here sympathetic to its ambitions. And like the same company towns, it saw that its own law officers were elected. Those of us who sold merchandise or services to the big Triangle H properties were content to vote in the men Triangle H wanted because much of our living depended on its favor. Lord Acton said: "All power corrupts and absolute power corrupts absolutely." We saw the exercise of that absolute power Monday.

What do we do about it?

We should ask the Commissioners for a special election to select a new sheriff, one that is beholden in no way to Triangle H. This newspaper does so now. The selection of a board of County Commissioners must wait until November's election. We should try to influence good men to run for that office, men who bear responsibility now and are willing to bear more. This is the only way we can erase the shame of last Monday.

Standing beside Kate's desk in the lamp-lit

Banner office, Jim folded this special edition of the *Banner* and looked down at Kate. She was exhausted, Jim saw, her hands ink-stained, a smudge of ink on her cheek and her hair awry from lack of attention. The clattering press in the rear made a racket hard to talk over.

"That says it, Kate," Jim said. "Come outside and we can talk."

Kate rose, and Jim, as he made his way to the counter gate, folded the paper and tucked it in the side pocket of his jacket. He held the gate open for Kate and they stepped out into the night. Kate sat down on one of the benches beside the door and leaned back against the many-paned window. She tilted her head back time and again to relax her neck and shoulder muscles, and Jim, standing above her, watched with sympathy.

"Nobody will love you for that editorial, Kate, but it needed saying."

"It's needed saying for ten years," Kate said wearily. She patted the bench beside her and Jim sat down. Away from the noisy press the night was quiet, and the heat left from the day's sun-baking of the street took some chill out of the night air. There was still the lingering smell of smoke from yesterday's fire.

Looking down the street, Jim could see no horse or wagon traffic at all. Under the light

of the River House door lamp, he saw three
men in conversation; otherwise the street was
empty except for his own tethered bay. It was
as if the town still cringed and hid from the
events of yesterday.

"You look tired, Jim."

"Puzzled, let's say. Too much has happened. I haven't caught up with it yet."

"What's to be done, Jim?"

"The district attorney and the marshal will
have to handle that one, Kate. Who knows what
bullets from what guns killed those eleven
men? Who fired the first shot at the cemetery?
And who fired the first one at the First
Chance? If I arrested every man involved, I'd
need two or three jails the size of the one we've
got. You can bet too, that any man who's sure
he killed another man will be long gone by the
time the marshal's here."

"Did you open your office today?"

"I spent some of the day talking with the
Judge and identifying corpses, and some of
the rest of the day making out warrants for the
arrest of everybody in those fights — those I
could remember, that is. That's in case the
marshal wants them. Then I had to handle the
string of barracks' lawyers. They wanted me
to organize everything from a lynch mob to a
posse." He paused, then added wryly, "Yesterday morning at seven-thirty, I was just a

pretty mad cattleman looking for the man who burned me out. Now I'm a reluctant sheriff, sleeping on an office cot and wondering what the hell will happen next."

"But you're still a pretty mad cattleman, aren't you?"

"Yes. And that reminds me." He turned to look at Kate, "Out at the cemetery this morning I was talking with Will-John, trying to stall the fight." He told Kate of Will-John's saying Jim should be leading the fight, since the nesters had burned him out. When asked how he knew about the burning of D Cross, Will-John had said Parker told one of his hands.

Kate straightened up and regarded his shadowed face, "Well, that's reasonable. After all, Parker's your nearest neighbor."

"Yes, except we don't get on. Burt Hethridge sold some range to me instead of leasing to him. He's never forgotten it. He wouldn't come on my range."

"Maybe he saw the fire."

"Then why doesn't the whole country know it? If Parker told a Triangle H hand, why wouldn't he tell other people? Why didn't they say something to me, in two days' time?"

"What are you getting at Jim?"

Jim said wearily, "I don't know. It's just strange that the word of any burn-out should come from Will-John. I reckoned I could track the first news of it back to a nester. Instead it came from Triangle H."

Kate was silent a long moment, pondering this, and then she said reasonably, "Riders are traveling this country all the time, Jim. Maybe one of them told Parker, or asked about the dead ashes at your place. Parker wouldn't know when it happened and would assume everybody knew about it. . . . I just don't know, either."

They were both tired, Jim knew, and as for himself, he knew he wasn't thinking clearly. He needed time and a clear head to reflect on this, and he was silent.

"Has Arly Green talked?" Kate asked.

Jim patted the *Banner* in his side pocket. "No. But when he sees your list, he might. You see, the men he's trying to protect are mostly dead. Oh, I forgot to tell you, Kate — some nester's young son stopped by after supper to tell me Beau Cather had died of gunshot wounds. Add him to your list."

Jim got up, saying, "I want to catch Arly while he's still awake. How much longer will you be at it?"

"An hour and a half probably. Then I'll go home and pick up the nightmares where they left off last night."

Kate rose too and she said, "Stop by in

the morning, Jim."

Impulsively, Jim put his arm around her shoulder and hugged him to her. What started out as a gesture of companionship, affection and shared troubles, turned into something else. Kate did not remain motionless, but turned to him, and Jim found himself folding her to him and putting his arms around her. For a still, surprised moment they looked at each other, and then Jim bent down and kissed her on the lips. It was only a second that Kate was unresponsive, then her lips parted and her body moved against his. They clung to each other for a sweet moment; then Kate moved back, her hands on Jim's chest.

Looking up at him, he could see the pleasure in her face. "I didn't expect that," she said slowly. "I mean I didn't expect to do that."

"Neither did I." He hesitated. "Are you sorry you did?"

Kate, hands still on his chest, rose on tiptoe and kissed him again, this time lightly. "That sorry," she said. "Good night, Jim."

She went back into the noisy shop, and Jim stood watching her until she had disappeared. A warm feeling of bewilderment and pleasure possessed him. These last two days, tense, strange and shocking, had thrown them much together, so that without consciously willing it each had become dependent on the other. Had he merely caught Kate at a time when she was physically weary, her guard down? Remembering her kiss, with its lightning stroke of passion, he didn't think so, and the second kiss proved it.

Smiling faintly in the darkness, he went over to his horse at the tie rail. Turning left on Bridge Street, he knew he was coming to the end of his pleasant reverie. Arly lay ahead of him.

When he let himself into his office in the courthouse he noted that somebody, perhaps the building's janitor, had made up his cot in the far corner, putting the blankets and pillow in order.

He went directly to his desk, reached in its lower drawer and brought out a half-full bottle of whiskey. Afterwards he put his hat on the desk top, got the cell keys from behind the door and went down to the cell block. He turned up the wick of the lamp in the corridor wall bracket and looked into Arly's cell. Arly was asleep, face to the wall, and Jim hesitated. Should he wait until tomorrow, or talk to him now?

The answer was that whatever mood Arly would waken to, the whiskey would make up for being roused.

Jim took the wall lamp out of its bracket,

tucked the bottle under his arm and moved over to the cell door and inserted the key. The sound of its turning roused Arly, and he slowly sat up, regarding Jim in sleepy puzzlement. He had taken off his pants and shirt and was sleeping in his filthy underwear.

"Now what?" he asked grumpily.

Jim locked the door, pocketed the keys and put the lamp on the floor beside the cot opposite Arly's. He took the bottle from under his arm and moved over to Arly's cot.

"Could you use some of this stuff, Arly?"

Arly looked at the bottle with suspicion. "What is it?"

"Store-bought whiskey, Arly. It's not the color you're used to drinking, but it's still whiskey."

"You must want somethin'."

"Just to talk with you." He held out the bottle and Arly took it. Pulling out the cork, he held it under his nose, and then smelled the contents of the bottle. Satisfied, he tilted the bottle and drank three deep swallows.

"Why don't you make it last awhile?" Jim asked. He drew the folded copy of the *Banner* from his pocket and said, "Arly, this is a copy of tomorrow's *Banner*. You want to read it or you want me to read it to you?"

Arly hesitated. "I don't read so good. Maybe you better read it."

Jim went over to the other cot, sat on it and unfolded the paper so that he could read it by the light of the lamp on the floor. Slowly and carefully he read what Kate had written. He didn't bother reading her editorial because he didn't want Arly's attention distracted from the news story.

When he looked up he saw that Arly was watching him intently, his mouth open, a look of disbelief on his face. He didn't speak for a moment, and then he said quietly, "So they got that bastard, Hethridge." Jim nodded, and Arly said, "Looks like I'm burned out."

"But you're alive. Plenty of others aren't."

"Read me that list again — them kilt and burned out."

"Before I read it to you, there's one more name to add. Beau Cather died last night and his neighbors buried him today." And Jim read the list again.

When he was finished, Arly said, "That must have been some fight I missed at O'Guy's." He added quietly, "Them murderin' bastards."

Jim folded the paper, put it on the blanket and moved back a little. Crossing his legs Indian fashion on the blanket, he hooked his thumbs in his belt and regarded Arly. "That list of dead men, Arly — that takes in most of the bunch that jumped Will-John Saturday night, doesn't it?"

Before answering, Arly took another drink. When he had caught his breath, he said slyly, "That's your guess. Me, I couldn't guess."

"You know what I think, Arly? I think you've kept your mouth shut about that Saturday night fight to protect your friends. Well, they're mostly gone. You can talk now without harm coming to them." He paused, watching Arly. "You could even claim you never wore a gun that night, Arly. There's nobody alive to say you did and put the blame on you."

Arly thought about this, looking down at the bottle cradled in his lap. Jim let him ponder before he spoke again. "Even if there's a man alive now who saw you packing a gun in that alley Saturday night, it's your word against his in court."

"Sure," Arly said absently. He was turning this over in his mind, looking for some advantage to himself, Jim guessed.

Jim said idly, "Now, like I said yesterday, Arly, you cooperate with the district attorney and he'll ask the Judge to go easier on you. I'm guessing there were five men in that bushwhack. I disarmed one, but I couldn't see who he was. Shorty and Beau are dead. Will you tell me what happened? You can leave that man's name out. We'll find him eventually, but you won't be blamed for it."

"Why are you so all-fired anxious to know?" Arly asked. "The ones that done it are dead."

"I'll tell you why, Arly. That night my house and building were burned to the ground. I think you know who did it."

A look of angry protest came to Arly's beard-stubbled face. "That's a damn lie! I never had nothing to do with it. I don't know anybody that even knows you was burned out! If they knew they'd of told me."

His surprise and protest seemed genuine to Jim, and he said, "Prove you didn't burn me out. What happened Saturday night?"

"You going to hang your fire on me?" Arly asked.

"I'm going to try unless you talk."

Arly thought about this a long moment, and then he said, "All right, God damn it, I'll tell you what happened! There was me and Shorty up on the roof of the Masonic Hall. Beau and Davy was in the alley and — that other feller you took the gun away from. It was Shorty got Martin, me that nicked Will-John before he took to the shed. I shot at the shed a couple of times before you opened up down in the alley. We thought it was that other feller shooting at the shed until you called to Will-John. We knew we had to get you out of there. I told Shorty I'd hold him by the arm while he leaned over so he could see you. When you hit him I had to leave go of him or else he'd have pulled me with him. Then I run."

"Ran where?"

"To back of O'Guy's where our horses was. Beau was there, shot in the belly. O'Guy and them others wanted to take him to Doc Purcell, but Beau wouldn't go."

"Why not?"

"He figured Doc couldn't do nothing for him. Besides, he was sure Triangle H would hunt him down at Doc's and kill him in bed. We all reckoned they would."

"All? How many?"

"Six — eight of us."

"Then what?"

"Well, we seen Will-John get hit. We figured he'd go to Doc's. Me and Prewitt was — " He caught himself and said, "Ah, hell, I done it."

"I didn't hear the name. Go on."

"Well, the rest of them was sure Triangle H would make a try for us that night. They wanted to take Beau home and fort up there. They left me and Prewitt to pick up Will-John when he come out of Doc's and watch him. If he went out to the Big House and rousted out the crew we knew we was in bad trouble. We was to ride back to Beau's place and tell 'em to get ready for 'em."

"Did you follow him?"

Arly nodded. "Him and Sarah Hethridge was in a buggy, and Cole and his missus was in the buckboard. They kept to the road but we cut out acrost country, left our horses and moved over to the crick and hid in the brush by the lake. They come in and a couple of hands come over and took their rigs back to the corral and unhitched. Will-John come back to his office. That's where he sleeps."

"How did you know that?"

Arly took a drink before he answered, "I never, but Prewitt did. The two hands come back after turning out the horses and went in the bunkhouse. It didn't look like nothing was going to happen and I wanted to go, but Prewitt said no. He said there was a door from Will-John's office into the bunkhouse. He said maybe Will-John could have went through that and be talking to the crew, getting ready to raid us. So we waited a while longer."

"Then what?"

"When they blowed the lamp in the bunkhouse, we figured everything was quiet for the night and we started for the horses, when something funny happened."

"Funny?"

"Yeah. Will-John come out of his office,

266

swung wide of the bunkhouse and went over to the corral."

"Wait a minute. How do you know it was Will-John?"

"Well, Doc had fixed him up with a sling for his arm. Seemed like all the lamps in the Big House were fired up and that give out enough light so you could pick up the white sling."

Jim uncrossed his legs and put his feet on the floor. "Then what, Arly?" he asked again.

"Will-John caught the morning horse out of the corral, rode him wide of the bunkhouse and walked him down around the lake. When he was past us, he crossed the crick and headed south. We figured that without him they wouldn't move, so we got our horses and rode back to Beau's."

South of the creek was the direction where D Cross lay. According to Arly's account, Will-John, in skirting the bunkhouse on his way to the corral and riding his horse toward the road, had been careful to be as quiet as possible. Why? Where was he headed for at that time on Saturday night? If he had been going to Number Two, which was somewhat south but more east, he would have kept to the road. If he had been aiming to scout the nesters, he would have kept to the road, too, for all of their places lay to the east of Triangle H.

As Jim turned these questions over in his mind, his curiosity altered into a faint, but beginning, suspicion. Arly could be lying about his and Prewitt's move that night, but Jim didn't believe he was. As described by Arly, every move he and his friends made that Saturday night were the actions of desperate and fearful men. It was logical for them to suppose that the serious wounding of Joe Martin (they couldn't know he was dead), and the slight wounding of Will-John would bring instant and vicious retaliation. Beau's place was closest to town and he was hurt badly, so there was every reason for them to hole up there. There was also good reason for them to put out Arly and Prewitt as watchers. If they were to be the prey, their best chance of survival was to stay together, not to scatter to watch for an attack; for by the time all the watchers could be called in the fight would be on and they could be attacked singly. With Arly and Prewitt out, they could remain together.

Moreover, if Arly was genuinely surprised at the news of the burning of D Cross — and Jim thought he was — he was not quick-thinking enough to make up this story on the spur of the moment. Up to now, it was only his story that suggested the possibility of Will-John's burning D Cross. Arly's beliefs were unstated, and Jim was sure that this possibility had not even occurred to him. To Arly, Jim Donovan was a Triangle H man, for hadn't he attacked Joe Martin's killers, and hadn't he been with Triangle H at Martin's funeral, and hadn't he arrested Arly for murder? It would never enter Arly's mind to accuse Will-John of the D Cross burning.

"Could any of your bunch have left Beau's place to burn D Cross?"

"Why, hell no! They was all there when we got back to Beau's. They wouldn't have had time to ride to your place and come back before we got back to Beau's."

That was true, Jim thought. But anyone of that crowd Saturday night who was sympathetic to the nester's cause could have started the fire. He tried to recall the men who had bid for the box suppers. He knew them all except for half a dozen punchers from outfits across the Cheat. But since none of the outfits over there had interests that conflicted with Triangle H's, there was no reason for them to seek revenge on a man they might think was a Triangle H partisan. No, there was no one in that crowd who would have fired his place.

One big question in his mind was unanswered. Why would Will-John, who was indebted to him for his rescue and badly wanted him to throw in with Triangle H, burn him out? Then it came to him with an almost suffocating certainty. *Will John wanted me to believe exactly what I did believe: that in retaliation for my killing one of the nesters, they had fired D Cross.* If, as Will-John believed that Saturday night, Jim was willing to listen to reason the following Sunday morning, wouldn't the nester burning of D Cross convince him he must throw in with Triangle H? Will-John had even made certain he wouldn't be at D Cross that night by suggesting he stay in town Saturday night and hit Triangle H on his way home next day, and Jim had agreed to this.

Now, real anger came to him. In something less than a week Will-John had acquired a wife, who brought with her half of Triangle H's wealth; he had seen Cole slaughtered; he had precipitated the showdown with the nesters by organizing the overlap of the times of the two funerals. If anyone was responsible for the ensuing fight and the burning of O'Guy's, it was Will-John; and he personally had burned D Cross — that, Jim was sure of now.

Arly's voice interrupted Jim's mental summation. "You goin' to arrest Prewitt?"

Jim stood up. "No, I got his gun before he got in trouble."

"Then if he ain't run, find him. Ask him about him and me Saturday night. He ain't a liar. If he knows he's helping me he'll tell you

270

the God's own truth."

Even now Arly didn't connect Will-John with the burning of D Cross, so intent was he on proving his own innocence.

"I'll do that, Arly."

Jim put the copy of the *Banner* in his pocket, picked up the lamp and let himself out of the cell. He locked the door behind him and put the lamp in its wall bracket. He said good night to Arly and was mounting the stairs when he remembered the whiskey. He didn't even break his stride at the memory. Half a quart of whiskey was a mighty small reward for the information Arly had given him this night.

19

Jim woke at three in the morning, and as he dressed in the dark of the sheriff's office he reviewed what he must do today. First, he must leave Arly without any breakfast, and very likely without a noon meal too. The same applied to himself, so why should he worry about Arly? He had a long ride ahead of him, but however long it was, he must be back at the cemetery for Cole's funeral. He wouldn't be dressed for it, but that didn't matter.

Strapping on his shell belt, he groped for his hat and found it and let himself out of the building. His horse, which had been grained last night, was stalled in the shed reserved for the sheriff's mount, and he whickered at Jim's approach. After saddling him up in the chill night, Jim mounted, turned right on Bridge Street and rode its length until he picked up the road south.

Last night, after leaving Arly, he had sat in the sheriff's office in the silent courthouse and tried to sort out what was important to him in

272

the happenings of these last few days. The three battles, the claims and counterclaims, the wrangling with the sheriff and his resignation, the identifying of bodies, the conference with the Judge, his own appointment as sheriff — all these belonged in a separate compartment. In his own mind, he wryly labeled them "in the public weal."

It was "the private weal," his own, with which he was concerned, and which he would act on next day. First, there was Arly's story of his and Prewitt's movements on Saturday night after the alley fight. Upon reflection, he was wholly convinced that Arly had been telling the truth. But as Arly had pointed out, to really cinch that truth he would have to find Prewitt to corroborate Arly's story. And that, Jim knew, would be next to impossible. The nesters had learned at the graveyard that he was a deputy sheriff; they would learn in today's *Banner* that he had been appointed acting sheriff.

That meant that Prewitt, who knew he would be wanted for participating in Saturday night's fight and Monday's cemetery battle, where Jim had spotted him both times, would head out of the country. There was nothing keeping him here except a few scrub cattle, since Triangle H had burnt him out along with the others. It could be a month, two months before he could catch up with Prewitt — and maybe it would be never.

Of far greater importance was what Will-John had told him before the cemetery battle. He had named Parker as the source of the information that D Cross was burned out, and Parker was available. His decision arrived at, Jim had gone to bed.

It was midmorning when he picked up Parker's turnoff, which was little more than a faint wagon track. Ahead of him, he could see the tops of the occasional cottonwoods that grew in the shallow valley of Limestone Creek, on whose banks Parker had established himself. Following the faint track, Jim rode on until he was in sight of Parker's place. It lay below him on the valley floor, a squat log cabin, a tiny barn-shed and a sagging pole corral. It was a mean place, somehow suited to the childless Parker and his gaunt Biblespouting wife. Putting his horse down the grade, Jim could hear the clanging of metal on metal, which suggested that Parker was doing some home blacksmithing.

When he reached the valley floor, Jim saw that the sound of blacksmithing was coming from the shed, whose double doors stood open. He put his horse through the weed-grown barn lot and reined up in front of the open doors. Looking from bright sunlight into the windowless shed, Jim could barely see the dim figure inside, and since the black-smithing continued, he guessed that Parker hadn't seen him. He dismounted, left his horse ground-haltered, and moved into the doorway. Parker, shirtless, but wearing a long-sleeved underwear shirt, was hammering at something he held on the anvil with tongs.

Not wanting to interrupt him while the metal was still hot, Jim waited until Parker had finished whatever it was he was fashioning and had thrown it into a wooden tub filled with water. Then he said, "Morning, Parker."

Parker whirled, sledge in hand. He was a broad, short man, without much flesh on his heavy-boned frame. His short-clipped grey-shot beard hid the lines of his ill-natured face. Under thick, greying eyebrows, below a stiff brush of grey hair, Jim could see the surprise in his muddy eyes.

"What are you doing on my place?" Parker asked in a surly voice.

"Just come to talk with you," Jim answered mildly.

Parker moved toward him, halted a short distance away and said, "We done our talking a long time ago. Ain't no more to say, so light out."

Jim put his shoulder against the door frame

and said, "I will, if you'll tell me a few things, Parker."

"Why should I, after what you done to me?"

Jim was silent for a long moment, watching him. There was no crack in his hostility, Jim saw, and he decided to act in a way he was reluctant to do.

"Well, for one thing, because I'm acting sheriff."

Parker squinched—his way, Jim supposed, of showing displeasure, disbelief, or even surprise.

"First I've heard of it."

"Been in town the last week?"

"Not for a month. Longer than that."

Jim reached in his pocket, drew out the star of the sheriff's office and held it in his palm for Parker to see.

Parker only grunted.

"Anybody you know been up this way lately, Parker?"

"Nope." Then he asked, "Like who?" Then, "You lookin' for somebody?"

Jim decided to duck that question. He asked instead, "You recollect last Saturday night, Parker?"

"Like any other. Why?"

"You didn't happen to look outside about one or two o'clock, Sunday morning, did you?"

"Why would I? I was asleep."

"Been up out of your valley or any place where you could see my place?"

"Nope. Why?"

"It was burned to the ground early Sunday morning."

Parker looked at him steadily, his mouth slacked open in surprise, and then he said, "And you think I done it?"

"You're the last one I'd think would do it, Parker. We've never held with each other's opinions, but I know you'd never do that. You're not that kind of man."

"Then what are you out here for?" Parker demanded.

Jim was silent a moment, considering Parker's answers to his questions. He was certain Parker hadn't known about the fire, for he was too simple a man to dissemble.

Again Jim parried the question. "Had any visitors since Sunday, Parker?"

"No. Not since the Sunday before that, and the Sunday before that." He added with quiet venom, "I ain't got any visiting neighbors, with you on one side of me and Triangle H on the other three sides."

"Do Triangle H riders ever drop by?"

"They know better," Parker said flatly. "Last one come here I drove him off with a rifle."

"When was that?"

"Year and a half ago."

"So you haven't seen or talked with a Triangle H rider since last Sunday?"

"You just heard me," Parker said.

Jim pushed away from the door frame, and said, "Thanks, Parker."

"For what?"

Jim smiled. "Well, I guess for not driving me off with a rifle."

Parker said unrelentingly, "I don't have one handy."

Jim moved out to his horse and mounted, waved to the bristly Parker standing in the doorway, who didn't wave back. Then he turned his horse and started across the barn lot. When he was even with the cabin, he glanced over and saw a bony, angular woman, dressed in black, standing in the doorway.

As he passed, she called, "Go and sin no more," in a cracked, mad voice.

Jim touched his hatbrim, and said, "I wouldn't think of it, ma'am."

As his horse climbed the gentle slope, Jim felt pity for the two half-mad people he had just left. Cross-grained, stubborn and hostile as he was, Parker had nevertheless given Jim the information he wanted.

Once on higher ground, Jim glanced at the position of the sun and knew that he was running late. He would miss the service for Cole at the church but, if he kept his bay at an alternate walk and trot, he could make the graveside ceremony.

As he rode on, he formulated one plan after another for his confrontation with Will-John, and discarded each. Always in the back of his mind was the fact of the Triangle H crew. Will-John had always had two or three of them siding him, and since Saturday night the whole crew seemed to form a bodyguard for him. Every Triangle H hand, except the guards Will-John would leave at the Big House and at Number Two, would be at Cole's funeral. After the funeral, they would hang around at the Cameo awaiting the mass burial of their dead comrades at four o'clock.

The legality of what he was about to do was doubtful, and any sheriff in his right mind, and one who wanted to be re-elected, would back away from it. Still, he thought wryly, perhaps he wasn't in his right mind, and certainly he didn't want to be elected.

When the cottonwoods of the distant Cheat loomed up, Jim headed straight for the westernmost group that marked the cemetery. As he came close enough to make out figures, he could see the procession of buckboards and riders following the black hearse as it entered the cemetery gates.

When he rode through these gates a few minutes later and took the lane toward the Hethridge burial plot, the service had already started. He dismounted, led his horse to the wrought-iron railing that surrounded one of the graves, and made his way among the tombstones and joined the large group at the graveside. Hat in hand, Jim quietly surveyed the crowd as the minister intoned the last rites.

Bonnie and Sarah, of course, were dressed in black and wore black hats and black veils. Will-John was wearing a dark townsman's suit, while the Triangle H crew behind them were dressed in their cleanest range clothes. The rest of the crowd was made up of ranch folk and the soberly dressed townsmen and their wives who had serviced Triangle H for many years. Some had even brought their children.

After the flowers were removed from the coffin, and the coffin lowered into the grave, the minister spoke the final prayer, tossed the dirt into the grave, and the ceremony was over. Now the townspeople crowded around Bonnie and Sarah to shake their hands in quiet commiseration. Jim, hat in hand, joined them. When he shook hands with Will-John, Sarah and Bonnie, he noted that the two women, damp handkerchiefs clutched in their left hands, were composed and gracious. Each gave him a small sad smile, one reserved for special friends on this sad occasion.

Afterwards, as he was walking back to his horse, he tried to analyze his feelings about Cole's death and burial. He could only sum them up in the thought that Cole's life had been an utter waste, and that now he was freed from the torment of living it.

The surrey was pulled up in the lane opposite the grave, and as Jim stood by his horse, watching, Will-John and the two women stepped into it and were driven off. Buggies and other vehicles followed, but not in procession. Jim mounted and let a few vehicles get between him and the surrey before he took to the lane. Where were they going now, he wondered. Will-John, of course, would wait in town for the later service. Would Sarah and Bonnie attend this service too? He doubted it. To have the foreman attend would observe the amenities, while the two women, having gone through one painful ceremony, could in the eyes of public opinion be excused from going through a second.

Jim kept the surrey in sight and saw it pull up at the River House, where Will-John handed down Bonnie and Sarah. All three went into the hotel.

The Triangle H crew, riding in a body,

turned at the River Street corner, and Jim guessed they were going down the half-block to the Cameo Saloon.

Jim waited until the surrey had pulled away, then put his horse at the tie rail by the River House portico. Entering the lobby, he guessed that the women had gone up to the suite Triangle H maintained at the River House. Will-John, he judged, would be at the bar, where most men could be found after a funeral.

When he entered the crowded barroom, Jim saw Will-John bellied up to the bar, and he moved over to a place beside him. Will-John had the *Banner* lying on the bar before him, and was reading Kate's story of "The Blackest Day." When Otey came up to him, Jim said, "A beer, Otey," and at the sound of his voice Will-John turned his head. His handsome face held a surly anger as he tapped the paper with his knuckles. "A pack of damn lies. If she was a man I'd take care of this."

"I don't find any lies in it. I thought it was as accurate as she could make it."

"They started the fight at the cemetery, and you know it."

"I don't know it. I was on top of Arly Green and never saw the first shot fired."

"Hell, didn't Arly start it?"

"It was at me, not you," Jim pointed out.

"Well, you stepped in Saturday night to save my neck. I tried to save yours."

Jim said mildly "I won't argue with you, Will-John. It's up to the district attorney and the marshal to untangle this."

"When are they coming?"

"Likely today. The marshal will have to come from Junction City. He'll probably pick up the district attorney on his way."

"Let 'em come," Will-John said grimly. "We got nothin' to hide."

"No, it was pretty much in the open," Jim said. He drank the glass of beer that Otey had brought him in long thirsty gulps, and set the glass down on the bar. "You got a few minutes free, Will-John?"

Will-John was pouring another shot of whiskey from the bottle in front of him. He finished pouring, and looked at Jim. "Sure, as soon as I get the taste of that funeral out of my mouth." He tossed off the whiskey in one gulp, and then said, "Ready."

"Let's go over to the courthouse. I've got Arly Green cooling off there."

Will-John scowled. "What's that stinking nester got to do with me?"

"I want you to hear his story, and then tell me what you think of it."

"What's his story?"

Jim pushed away from the bar, saying, "He'll tell you."

He started for the lobby and he heard Will-John fall in behind him. They went out to the boardwalk and halted under the portico. "You afoot?" Jim asked.

Will-John tilted his head in the direction of the river. "My horse is over there."

They parted and Will-John crossed the road to the shady cottonwoods, while Jim went over to his bay and mounted. He watched Will-John reach his horse, tighten the cinch and mount, and then they joined, riding up River Street.

At the courthouse Will-John waited in the corridor while Jim unlocked the door to the sheriff's office and got the cell keys. Jim led the way down the steps.

Arly, hearing the footsteps, was already at the cell door, grasping its bars. When he saw Jim, he said angrily, "God damn it! Don't you feed your prisoners? I ain't had — " Arly's voice trailed off as he saw Will-John Seton behind Jim.

"I know, Arly," Jim said. "I haven't eaten either."

Arly was watching Will-John, hatred in his eyes, and now he said softly, "Tell me I'm right. Tell me you're goin' to lock up that bastard."

Jim was about to use the cell keys, and then he thought better of it. It was just as well to keep bars between those two, he thought.

Will-John halted in the middle of the stone-floored corridor in front of Arly's cell. "If I didn't know who you had locked up here, Jim, I could tell it by the smell."

"All right," Jim said. "Both of you let me do the talking. Arly, go sit on your cot."

Scowling, Arly moved back and sat on the edge of the cot. Jim went over to the side wall and put his back against it, where he could watch both men. "Now, Arly," he begin, "I want you to tell me again what you did after the fight in the alley Saturday night. Start with meeting your bunch at O'Guy's after the fight."

Arly was silent a moment thinking this over. Jim knew he was wondering if the repetition could get him in any more trouble.

Apparently Arly didn't think so, and he began to talk. Jim was watching Will-John's face as Arly told about the nesters deciding that Will-John should be followed to see if he was going to collect the whole crew for a night raid on them. He told of himself and Prewitt following the buggy and buckboard to the edge of town, circling wide and cutting across country to the Triangle H. Will-John's expression was one of boredom as Arly went on to tell of them hiding their horses in a shallow arroyo and proceeding on foot to their hiding spot in the alders below the lake.

Arly told of seeing Will-John entering the bunkhouse after talking with Sarah, and of his own conviction that once the bunkhouse lamps were put out the threat of a night raid was over. But Prewitt, he said, wanted to wait even after the hands who had turned out the teams returned to the bunkhouse and the lamps were doused. They were headed for their horses, Arly said, when they saw Will-John coming out of the bunkhouse, go to the corral, saddle a horse and quietly ride down the road past where they had been hiding and then cross the creek, heading south.

As Will-John listened, he took a step closer to Arly, his expression intent. When Arly finished, Will-John looked at him and said "What am I supposed to say, except that it's a damn lie? Even if I did what he said, how could they tell it was me in the dark?"

"Tell him, Arly," Jim said.

"You were wearing that sling. That showed up good."

"You think after gettin' shot at, gettin' hit and losin' blood that I'd go for a night ride? I'm not that crazy. I think you're makin' it up, Arly."

"Why would he make it up?" Jim asked.

"Why, to get me in trouble."

"What other trouble was there Saturday night that I could get you into?" Arly asked.

Jim said mildly, "You haven't caught it yet have you Arly?"

"Caught what?"

"Why, that's the night my place was burned to the ground. Remember?"

Arly looked at him in slack-jawed wonder, and then his glance shifted to Will-John, and in his expression was the beginning of comprehension.

Jim looked at Will-John now. "I talked with old Parker this morning, Will-John. You said he told one of your hands I was burned out. Parker hasn't talked to one of your men for a year and a half. So, how did you know I was burned out, if you didn't set the fire yourself?"

Arly cut in then. "You mean he burned you?"

Jim looked steadily at Will-John. "Did you?"

Will-John's face held a cold fury as he said to Arly, "You sneaky bastard! You tried to kill me Saturday night and now you're trying to lie me into jail! You're lying, Arly! You made the whole thing up!"

"I see it now, you double-crossing son of a bitch," Arly said. "You burned down his place so he'd think we done it. You figured he'd throw in with you after that didn't you? You figured — "

Will-John's hand went toward his gun, and Jim, a fraction of a second later, went for his. Will-John didn't bother to sight on Arly; he shot from the hip.

The sound in the room was deafening, but in that sound was the clang of metal, and afterwards, the brief whine of a ricochet and the splat of a bullet against stone. Jim's gun was clear now, and he knew, since Arly was still standing, that Will-John's bullet had hit one of the cell bars and been deflected.

"Drop it, Will-John!"

Will-John didn't even hear him. When Jim heard the click of Will-John's gun being cocked, Jim aimed at his legs and fired.

The impact of his slug wiped Will-John's feet out from under him and he fell heavily. His gun skittered out of his hand against the cell bars and stopped.

Moving swift as thought, Arly lunged for the free gun, and Jim called, "No, Arly, no!"

He swung his gun toward Arly and found himself so close to the cell bars that the line of them almost made a wall screening Arly. It was as if he were at the end of a picket fence, where his position made the fence seem solid.

Arly reached through the bars and got the

gun and Jim shot at the hand lifting it. He missed, and before he could cock his gun Arly pumped two quick shots into Will-John's body two feet away. Then Arly dropped the gun, and Jim took two quick steps to where he could see Arly clearly.

Arly said, with almost a lilt in his voice, "He shot at me first. I shot at him second. You seen it yourself, Sheriff."

20

Billy Arnold from the *Banner's* back doorway watched the hearse pull up in the alley by the steps of Woodward's loading platform next door. Billy was twelve years old, bright and thoroughly knowledgeable. Since he was at the source of the printed news, and paid attention to it he knew the mass funeral for the Triangle H crew would take place in an hour. Simple curiosity made him wonder if Hank Woodward would take all four coffins in one load, or make two trips with two coffins each time. He watched as Woodward and one of his employees stepped down from the hearse and came around to open the rear doors before loading the coffins.

When the doors opened, he saw Woodward turn his back to the hearse, grasp something in each hand and move slowly forward. Woodward's young man then reached out and also grasped something shielded by Woodward's body. They turned toward the steps and Billy saw they were carrying a stretcher that held a body covered with clean canvas. *Another?* Billy thought with amazement as he watched the two men stagger up the steps and vanish into the rear room of the hardware store. He waited, and presently Woodward and his companion came out with the first coffin.

Billy turned and walked back through the silent shop wanting to tell Rich what he had seen, and then he remembered Rich had gone off for a beer. Kate was sitting at her desk, and Billy, bursting with his news, came up to the railing.

"Miss Kate, guess what I just seen."

"Saw, Billy," Kate corrected him, and looked up from what she was writing.

"I just saw Hank Woodward and Bernie Banks take a dead men out of the hearse."

Kate frowned. "Did you see who it was?"

"No, ma'am. He was covered with canvas."

Kate stood up and walked around the desk, kneed the gate open and went back through the shop, Billy trailing her.

When she reached the back door and looked out, she saw Woodward and his young man loading a pine box into the hearse. She stepped out into the alley and walked toward them. Woodward turned and started for the steps, when Kate called out, "Wait a minute, Hank."

Woodward, dressed in his sober funeral

clothes, halted and waited until Kate came up to him.

"Billy said you just brought in a body."

Woodward nodded. "Will-John Seton's."

Kate held her stunned silence for long seconds, and then she asked, "What happened, Hank?"

"It was in the jail cell. Will-John and Jim were talking to Arly Green — I never found out what about. Will-John tried to shoot Arly, but his bullet hit one of the cell bars. Jim shot Will-John in the legs and knocked him down. He dropped his gun and Arly reached through the bars and got it. Arly shot him twice."

"Did — did Jim shoot Arly?"

Hank shook his head. "No, Arly dropped the gun right away." He added grimly, "Why not? He'd got the job done."

Without another word Kate turned and went back into the *Banner* building. When she reached her desk she sagged into the chair, trying to drive a kind of numbness from her brain.

Why had Jim brought Will-John to confront Arly? And why had Jim let Arly do it?

Then the full horror of Jim's day came to Kate. It was Jim would have to tell Sarah and Bonnie of Will-John's killing. It was Jim too, who would have to tell the Triangle H crew of the death of their boss. As she sat there her heart aching for Jim, she heard the Primrose stage roll by, going to the River House to unload its passengers.

Numbly, Kate rose, went out the front door and turned toward the River House. When she reached the corner the passengers had already descended from the coach and were waiting, loosely grouped while the driver lifted out their baggage from the boot.

She saw a short stout man in townman's clothes talking to a taller man, on whose shirt was pinned a badge. She recogized the district attorney, Sam Abel, and the man he was talking to was undoubtedly a U. S. Marshal.

Kate walked slowly back toward the *Banner* office and, no matter how she fought them back, tears came into her eyes. Jim would leave weeping women to confront angry men, only to meet with these two men, who probably held the view that Jim should never have allowed any of the past week's slaughters to happen.

She ached to be with him in all his confrontations, and knew she couldn't be with him in any of them. There was one thing she could do, though, and she hurried into the *Banner* office and to her desk. Standing there, she wrote a note which read: *Jim, come to my house when you can, no matter what time. Kate.* Folding it, she went back through the shop, where

Billy was standing in the door.

"Billy, ask Mr. Woodward for a ride out to the cemetery. I want you to give this note to Jim Donovan. If he isn't there, find him."

"Where?"

"I don't know," Kate said impatiently. "Take the afternoon off and find him. The cemetery, the courthouse, the hotel, his office. I don't know where, but find him."

It was well after nine o'clock that night when Kate, reading in the living room at home, heard footsteps on the porch. The bell rang when she was halfway across the room. Opening the door, she saw Jim's figure outlined against the night.

"Evening, Kate."

She noted instantly the dragging weariness in his voice and she stepped aside, saying, "Come in, Jim, where I can see you."

He followed her into the living room, and she turned to look at him. He looked beat, angry and sad. Kate held out her hand for his hat, and said, "Sit down, Jim. Is a drink in order?"

"Yes." Then he smiled faintly. "That's a command, Kate."

Kate went to the kitchen, where a lamp was already burning, got a bottle of whiskey, two glasses and a pitcher of water, put them all on a tray and returned to the living room. Jim was stretched out in the deep easy chair, legs straight out, head back, eyes closed. He roused when Kate put the tray on the table beside him. She poured his drink and as she handed it to him, he asked, "You know about Will-John don't you?"

Kate nodded. "I don't understand any of it, Jim. Not even why he was at the jail."

She sat down and Jim began talking, his voice tired and bitter. He told her of his conversation with Arly Green last night and of Arly's revelation that he and Prewitt Saturday night had seen Will-John secretly leave Triangle H after the fight and head south. The suspicion had been planted in his mind then, Jim said, so that this morning he had ridden out to talk with Parker and found that Will-John had lied when he said Parker had told one of the Triangle H hands that D Cross was burned out. That, Jim said, was his reason for bringing Will-John to the jail for a confrontation with Arly. Arly's story, plus Jim's proof that Will-John had lied about Parker, had fired Will-John's wrath beyond control. Will-John's death at Arly's hands was a freak. Jim shot Will-John in the legs, hoping only to disarm him so he could stand trial for, among other things, the burning of D Cross. But Arly saw his chance with the gun, pounced on it and Jim's shot to forestall him had missed. Arly's hadn't, and his two quick shots killed Will-John.

"Shooting at Arly was Will-John's admission of guilt, then?"

Jim nodded, and then took a sip of his drink.

"Did you see Bonnie and Sarah?" she asked.

Again Jim nodded, and said, "Sarah fainted. Bonnie came at me like a tiger and then broke down completely. It was as if Will-John was *her* husband, not Sarah's. I called the housekeeper and got out."

"You went to the cemetery?"

"I went," Jim said grimly. "I told them Will-John was dead and that the U. S. Marshal was expected on today's stage. I said everyone of them, except the guards, could be charged with murder or arson, or both. I told them if they had the sense they were born with, they'd get out of the country before the marshal could move." He smiled wryly. "They didn't even wait for the funeral ceremony. They didn't even talk it over. They just rode out."

"Was it the truth you told them, Jim?"

"Yes, but I didn't know it then. That's what Marshal Burrows planned, and he wasn't very happy about my warning them. He wasn't very happy either about my letting Will-John into the cell block with a gun."

"Will they do anything to you?"

"No. When Burrows and Abel cooled down, they saw that warning the crew would save them months, maybe years of investigation and prosecutions they had a damn poor chance of winning."

Kate was silent a moment. "What's going to happen to the two women, Jim?"

Jim said quietly, "The old Triangle H is finished, Kate. A lot of that range is patented land, so it can be sold. The open range will be moved in on by other cattlemen. If I were Bonnie and Sarah, I'd put the land and stock up for sale. They'd not come out of it poor."

"What about you, Jim? Your place is gone. You could sell everything and move, like Bonnie and Sarah."

Jim looked at her searchingly, and Kate was immediately sorry she had said what she had. Jim rose, put his glass on the tray and started a slow circle of the room as he began to talk.

"No, with Triangle H gone, the best part of living here is ahead for us. I am going to try for a chunk of Triangle H land when it goes up for sale. I'm going to build a new house, a big house with room enough for a wife and a raft of kids."

Kate said, "You sound as if you're planning

your wife's life without even consulting her."

Jim halted in front of her, and looked down at her. "Why, who do you think I'm talking to?" he asked, and put out his hands to draw her up to him.

L
Short, Luke, 1908–1975.
Donovan's gun T135L

92